Whatever Happened to Virginia Dare

A Search for the Lost Colony

www.mascotbooks.com

Whatever Happened to Virginia Dare

The cover photograph of the original "Dare Stone" is used by permission of Brenau University only for purposes of a realistic illustration for a work of fiction.

For more information, please contact:
Mascot Books
560 Herndon Parkway #120
Herndon, VA 20170
info@mascotbooks.com

Library of Congress Control Number: 2016916322
CPSIA Code: PRBVG1216A
ISBN-13: 978-1-68401-008-0

Whatever Happened to VIRGINIA DARE

A Search for the Lost Colony

A Novel By

Lee Dorsey

OTHER PUBLISHED BOOKS BY LEE DORSEY

A Forbidden Love

Indiscretions

The Artist

Androgyny

Mercenaries of Panama (Frank the Survivor)

Mercenaries of Panama (Shada)

A Search for Love

The Triangulum Galaxy

This novel is dedicated to my cousin (sister)
Joyce Frock Phelps
who loves early American History

Acknowledgments

I would like to thank Professor Philip S. McMullan, Jr.
Who shared his in-depth knowledge and research on "The Lost Colony"

And

Deborah Thompson, Center for Greek Life and Campus Traditions
David Morrison, Vice President for Communications and Publications
Brenau University
For allowing me access to the Elinor Dare Stone

Whatever Happened to Virginia Dare is a novel about the early history of the English attempting a first settlement in 16th century America. The reader has to remember that the following pages are based on many facts as they are known and an exercise of my imagination. In other words, much of what you'll read here actually happened according to the historical records and some of it did not. This novel was not written as an historical thesis, but rather to entertain the reader. I hope that you enjoy reading this story as much as I did in writing it.

Lee Dorsey (Author)

CHAPTER I

On the morning of April 27, 1584, two clinker-built ships owned by Sir Walter Raleigh, the Ark Royal and the Mary Spark were anchored in the Portsmouth Harbor. The morning air was softly depositing spring pollen across the ships' decks as the water lapped against their sides from the incoming tide. The ships were fully loaded with supplies, ammunition, and a complete complement of crew members. The previous night, a company of soldiers were divided between both vessels and bedded down for the night.

The crew had been up early to prepare the ships for leaving with the afternoon outgoing tide. Everyone aboard was anxious to get underway. Their mission was to intercept a Spanish galleon that had been reported by British intelligence leaving Santo Domingo two days hence. According to the report, the ship was loaded down with gold and jewels, a port in Spain its destination.

The captains of the Ark Royal (Philip Amadas) and the Mary Stark (Arthur Barlowe) had been given permission by Queen Elizabeth to intercept this Spanish galleon and sail it back to England along with the contraband. The Queen had indicated that ten percent of the spoils would be divided among the crew and each captain would receive three percent for their trouble. Sir Walter

Raleigh would receive five percent and the Crown would reimburse Raleigh for any damages that the ships might receive during the anticipated sea battle. Everyone aboard both ships was happy and agreeable with the arrangement.

Around two hours after dawn as Captain Amadas sat at his desk studying charts of the Atlantic Ocean, a knock was heard at the door.

Without looking up from the charts that he was studying, he said in a loud voice, "Enter!"

The cabin door opened and his first mate Thomas Berns said, "Captain, Mr. Barlowe and several gentleman have come alongside in a jolly boat and are proceeding to come aboard, sir."

"Thank you, Mr. Berns. Have our visitors come directly to my cabin."

The first mate left and proceeded back on deck. Amadas began to roll up the charts that he had been studying and within several seconds a knock was heard again at the door.

"Enter, please!" Captain Amadas said. He stood up from behind his desk to greet the visitors.

The first to enter was Captain Arthur Barlowe followed by three distinguished gentlemen.

"Captain Barlowe, please do the introductions," Amadas said as he extended his hand in a welcoming gesture.

"I would like to introduce you to Simon Fernandez who is a chief pilot by trade."

"It's my pleasure, Mr. Fernandez," Amadas said.

Barlowe turned to John White and said, "John is a famous artist who has traveled with the Queens Navy around the known world and has sketched wonderful pictures of foreign lands. John is scheduled to sail with Richard Granville's ship to America in a few months to make maps and explore the coast line.

Amadas and White shook hands.

Amadas said, "Yes, I've seen your work. You are very talented, sir."

White responded, "Thank you sir for the compliment."

"And this is Thomas Harriot. Mr. Harriot" Barlowe said, "is a resident mathematician and intellectual at the Queens court."

Barlowe slightly paused, and with some hesitation said, "I have received a direct order from Sir Humphrey Gilbert on behalf of Sir Walter Raleigh who has been given a six year charter from the Queen to immediately explore and settle on her behalf, unclaimed portions of North America and to convert the natives to the Protestant faith."

He took another pause before he said, "We have been directed to take on this mission in the name of the Queen. Unfortunately, we are not going to intercept the Spanish galleon, but we're to sail directly west to the North American coast and survey it for the possibility of establishing a colony. Richard Grenville's ship will be following us in a month or so with metallurgists and explorers to determine the location of valuable metals. The Queen has indicated in this document that she will handsomely reward the crews and officers of both ships when they return to England in a year's time."

Barlowe set the document down and Amadas looked at the desk as if to collect his thoughts. After a few moments, "I can't say that I'm not disappointed. However, if Sir Walter wishes that we change the mission and the Queen has commanded it, we will do our duty."

Barlowe spoke next. "Mr. Fernandez will remain behind after we leave and he'll go over the charts with you to plot our course to America. He has extensive experience sailing with Francis Drake along the coast of America, and has some good information as to where in America would be a good location to begin a colony."

Amadas picked up the charts he had been previously studying and handed them to Fernandez who unfurled the charts on the desk and began to study them.

Barlowe said that he would escort Harriot back to his ship and settle him into quarters. "Captain, you will be the lead ship with Mr. Fernandez plotting our course. Please make arrangements to place him into some comfortable quarters when he finishes his work with you," Barlowe said.

Amadas nodded his head in a positive direction. Barlowe, White and Harriot bowed their heads to Amadas as they turned and left the cabin.

Once Barlowe and company left, Amadas turned to Fernandez and said, "If you'll excuse me sir, I want to muster the crew on deck and inform them of the change in the mission."

Fernandez looked up from the charts that he had been briefly studying and nodded his head in agreement.

Amadas left the cabin and walked up onto the deck. He stepped up onto the deck at the rear of the ship and called to his first mate, "Mr. Berns! Call the crew to assemble on deck; I have some important information to relay."

Mr. Berns moved about the ship and rounded up the crew and the contingency of soldiers who had arrived the night before. Within minutes the entire ships company were looking up at Captain Amadas anticipating his words.

For a moment the Captain stood looking down at the eager faces staring up at him.

"Gentlemen, most of you have served with me for the last two years. The mission we had planned to embark on today was to intercept the Spanish galleon that was reported to leave the harbor at Santo Domingo. It was also reported that she was loaded down with jewels and gold and the take would have resulted in big rewards for all of us."

He took another pause. "I was informed a few minutes ago that

that mission has been cancelled."

There was a low moan throughout the crew.

"The Queen has directed us on an even more important mission that is in the best interest of the country and Crown. We have been ordered to sail for America and lay the ground work for an English colony."

Another slight moan went up among the crew when they heard these last words from the Captain.

"I know that you are all disappointed with this change of mission, but we have our orders and to the man I expect you to carry them out. The Queen has assured me that we will be generously rewarded for our work."

Amadas took another pause and smiled, "Men, once our work has been completed in America, I will take some time to intercept any Spanish caravels that we may encounter on their route to Spain."

The gathered crew cheered..

"That's all I have to say. Now, get back to your duties and prepare the ship to leave with the tide. Thank you for your understanding and attention." Amadas stepped down from the upper deck and walked back into the cabin.

As Amadas opened the cabin door Fernandez looked up from the chart that he was studying. "Captain, come in please. I want to briefly go over the route to America that I am going to recommend."

Amadas moved to the other side of the desk and addressed his attention on the chart.

Fernandez pointed to an area in the middle of the chart and said, "That is the island of Sao Miguel, and on this side of that island is Porta Delgada. Although this island is under the ownership of the Portuguese, they are very receptive to any business that comes their way. I would suggest that we spend a few days there; we can resupply and it will give the crew time to relax. Once we leave that port, it is more than fifteen hundred miles to the coast of America. As you know, once we reach our destination, the work that the crew will undertake will be strenuous as well as dangerous. Although it's been my experience sailing the American coast with Francis Drake, the natives appear to be friendly, but we have to remember, they are savages and can change without any provocation."

Amadas took a moment and studied the chart. He turned to Fernandez and said, "Sir, once we leave port and sail into the ocean, I will turn over the ship to you for navigational purposes. Now sir, I will have my first mate show you to your quarters. We will be leaving anchorage in two hours. I will call you when we are about to enter the Atlantic Ocean."

Fernandez extended his hand to Amadas and they shook in friendship. Amadas called to Mr. Berns. Almost immediately, Berns entered the cabin.

"Mr. Berns, please show Mr. Fernandez to his cabin."

"Mr. Fernandez if you'll follow me," Berns said.

Berns opened the door and allowed Fernandez to pass and leave the cabin as he followed. Amadas sat down behind the desk and studied the chart and Fernandez's markings.

CHAPTER II

Captain Amadas and Mr. Berns stood on the aft deck and looked down at the crew. Mr. Berns shouted "Aweigh the anchor." The crew went into action. The anchor was aweigh as the sails were unfurled and the Ark Royal slowly began to leave the Portsmouth harbor, followed closely by the Mary Spark.

When the two ships reached the mouth of Portsmouth Harbor, they made a slow but definite left turn into the English Channel and then proceeded into a westerly heading. They were now about an hour's sail down the channel where it emptied into the Atlantic Ocean.

The movement of the ship awakened Mr. Fernandez, so he came onto the deck. He took his place alongside of Amadas and Berns. After a moment, he commented, "We have good weather to begin our adventure."

The rest of the hour passed by while the crew attended to their duties under the observations of Mr. Berns who periodically made comments to individual crew members in a loud and stern voice.

It wasn't long before the channel widened and the Atlantic Ocean came into view. The ships sailed several miles into the Atlantic, past the island of Jersey and the isle of Guernsey. These islands were to be the last land these men would encounter for the next thousand miles.

A wind out of the northeast filled their sails and each ship was doing a steady twelve knots. The Mary Spark moved as close to the Ark Royal as she possibly could without putting her bow into her stern.

It was early spring and daylight was at a premium. Before darkness finally fell, Captain Amadas had a line attached to the Mary Spark in an effort that the ships would not get separated during the night. There was a generous length of line extended to prevent a collision. Both captains recorded the day's activities into their logs.

As the days passed, everyone aboard both ships was doing their routine duties and both crews were assigned watch during the long nights. Mr. Fernandez never stopped studying the charts, studying the stars, and taking readings at noon each day. He always ensured periodically that the compass needle was glued on a south westerly course.

Four weeks into the sail one of the crewmembers who had been on watch in the early morning hours shouted, "Land ho!"

They were two miles off the Coast of Sao Miguel Island and as they moved closer, Porta Delgada came into view.

There was a lot of excitement among the crew, since they were aware they were going to be on leave for the next few days while the ships were resupplied.

The Ark Royal led the way into the harbor where she dropped anchor two hundred yards off the shore. The Mary Spark glided by and dropped her anchor a few hundred feet away.

As the crews of both ships were moving about their respective decks and securing the anchorage, a jolly boat was launched from the shore and headed in the direction of the two ships. When they were within shouting distance, one of the Portuguese in the jolly boat called out to the Ark Royal and requested they be allowed to come aboard. Captain Amadas who was standing by the rail shouted,

"Please gentlemen, come aboard and join us for lunch."

As the jolly boat was a few feet from the Ark Royal, two of the crewmembers lowered a rope ladder over the side. One of the men in the jolly boat tossed a rope to one of the crewmembers to secure the jolly boat. As the men began ascending the rope ladder, the crewmembers assisted the men in climbing aboard.

A jolly boat from the Mary Spark approached the other side of the Ark Royal. Aboard were Captain Barlowe and his first mate, John Harris. Once the jolly boat was secured Captain Barlowe and John Harris came aboard.

Captain Amadas introduced himself and Captain Barlowe to the Portuguese delegation that identified themselves as Joao de Macedo and Duarte Correa.

Everyone was escorted by Amadas to his cabin. Mr. Berns was directed to have a crew-member come in and prepare a table for lunch. Barlowe had brought with him a bottle of expensive wine to serve to the guests. After everyone's glass was filled Amadas suggested that everyone sit down at the table.

Since all of the English and Portuguese were fluent in Spanish, they agreed to communicate in that language.

After a few minutes of silence, Duarte asked the first question, "What is your destination, gentlemen?"

Barlowe was the first to answer: "We are at the direction of the Queen of England. Our destination is America to determine the feasibility of establishing a small settlement there and trade with the natives of that land."

Joao spoke next: "Gentlemen, you are educated men and therefore you must know that many years ago, the Pope decided that the New World was to be divided between the Portuguese and the Spanish. He drew a line from pole to pole and any land of the continent of America on the east of the line was to become land owned by the Portuguese, and to the right of the line, the Spanish. We named our land Brazil and as we speak, are in the process of developing it. I feel an obligation to tell you that the Spanish, when they learn of your intentions to establish a colony on their land in America, will have every intention of attacking you."

Captain Amadas spoke up, "Gentlemen, and with no disrespect to your religion, we don't recognize that the Pope had the authority to give away land that wasn't his. As best as we can determine, America is a very big place and there is enough land for every country that wants to establish a colony there to do so."

Barlowe spoke up and said, "Our destination is not Brazil; therefore, we are not intruding on land that is claimed by the Portuguese. We also know that the relationship between the Portuguese and Spanish governments is strained, but England and Portugal have good trade relations." He raised his glass of wine and made a toast, "To the friendship between Portugal and England."

They touched their glasses and repeated the toast. At that moment, three crew members brought in trays of food and placed them on the table.

After everyone filled their plate with the food, Captain Amadas informed the Portuguese that they only intended to stay for a few days and purchase supplies for the last leg of their sail.

"We would like your permission to allow our crews to come ashore in small groups in an effort to give them a chance to relax before they go back to the grinding duties of operating the ships."

"As long as they behave themselves and respect our women they will be welcome. However, if there is an incident of any kind you'll be asked to leave immediately," Duarte said.

"You have our word as gentlemen that if any of our crew

members misbehave, we will allow you to deal with them under the Portuguese judicial system," Barlowe said.

"Gentlemen, I know our visit here will be beneficial to all. Now allow me share with you a few bottles of wine from my personal stock." Amadas stood and retrieved two more bottles of vintage wine from a rack in the corner of the cabin.

The men continued to eat their lunch and drink the wine. The atmosphere was friendly and amicable.

After two hours of dining, the Portuguese delegation left the Ark Royal and rowed their jolly boat back to shore. Barlowe and Amadas retired to the cabin to discuss their stay in the harbor and requested the presence of Fernandez.

The next half hour was spent going over the final leg of the mission. Fernandez explained to the captains that the land they will initially come upon in America is a long stretch of islands with the ocean on one side and a bay on the other.

The one time he sailed along that land mass, he noticed what he believed to be an island in the middle of the bay. He said that when they reach the first land mass their challenge will be to find an inlet to enter the bay from the ocean. He said that he saw at least two breaks in the outer islands when he was sailing with Francis Drake, but he wasn't sure how navigable those openings were to allow the ships entrance to the bay.

"We will deal with that problem when we are confronted with it," Amadas said.

Barlowe concurred with Amadas assessment. The three had another glass of wine, and then the captains agreed to address their respective crews before they were allowed ashore.

Barlowe and his first mate, Mr. Harris, rowed back to the Mary Spark in their jolly boat. Captain Amadas had Mr. Berns call the crew together so he could address them. In the meantime, he climbed onto the upper deck on the rear of the ship and looked down as the crew gathered and looked up at him.

"Men, I don't have to remind you that we are guests of the Portuguese in this harbor. I have given them my solemn promise that when you go ashore for your respite, you will conduct yourselves as English gentlemen. You are not to commingle with the Portuguese women, and you will conduct your behavior at all times as a diplomat representing your Queen and country. If it is reported to me that any one of you does not conduct yourselves in the most gentlemanly manner, I will leave you here and allow the government of this island to deal with you."

"Now," Amadas said, "with a shake of your heads in the affirmative, assure me that you understand every word I just spoke to you."

All of the crew on the deck moved their heads up and down.

"Good! Now Mr. Berns will assign small groups shore leave in four hours intervals. If you arrive back late from your leave, you will be assigned extra duty once we get underway."

Amadas then looked down at the assembled crew and said, "That will be all for now, so return to your duties." The captain stepped down and followed by Mr. Berns, he went back to his cabin.

Amadas walked around behind his desk and sat down. "Mr. Berns," he said, "I want you to take several men ashore and have them fill up the water casks and then return them to the ship. When you return, inform me what the Portuguese have for sale in their market. I believe that we are in need of some salt pork to sustain us for the rest of the voyage."

"Captain, I will speak with Mr. Harris when he comes ashore to fill up their water casks. Maybe the two of us can barter a better price if we purchase the food supplies together."

"That's good thinking, Mr. Berns. Report back to me when you return."

"Aye, Captain," he responded. And then he turned and left the cabin.

Once back on deck, Mr. Berns ordered casks brought from below and the jolly boat lowered and with six crewmen, they loaded four casks onto the jolly boat and rowed to shore. There was a pier jetting out about twenty-feet from the shoreline. They tied up their jolly boat to the pier and proceeded directly into the market.

The crew of the Ark Royal took note of the young attractive women working at the various kiosks. Mr. Berns noticed the crew's reaction to these beauties and was determined not to allow any of his men out of his sight. He kept them in a tight formation. Stopping at one of the kiosks manned by an elderly Portuguese man, he asked in Spanish for directions to the water source on the island.

He learned from that conversation that the fresh water on the island was drawn from a waterfall and stream a mile and half inland. The man pointed in the direction of where the water could be found. Mr. Berns and his crew marched off in that direction.

After walking what seemed like five miles, the sound of water passing swiftly nearby could be heard. The four casks were filled with fresh water and a crewman on each side of the cask took hold of ropes that were attached and began their long trek back to the shoreline.

Hauling the water for over an hour and a half exhausted the men. They loaded the water casks into the jolly boat and rowed back to the ship.

Once they arrived back at the ship, the water was hoisted onto the deck and then was stored below. More empty casks were brought on deck for another detail of crew to be sent to retrieve water. The crew members that had retrieved the first rations of water were allowed to take a second jolly boat and go ashore for a respite. One of the senior members of the crew was put in charge of the group to ensure they didn't get into any trouble.

The next day, Mr. Berns and Mr. Harris took a detail of men ashore for the purpose of purchasing food supplies. Once ashore they went from kiosk to kiosk bargaining, and they eventually settled on the one kiosk that was offering the lowest price. For each ship, they purchased five hundred pounds of salt pork, two hundred pounds of grain and three hundred pounds of nuts that were grown on the island.

Captain Barlowe and his men made their rounds, filling their water casts and bringing their food supplies aboard. Men from the Mary Stark followed suit loading their ship.

On the third afternoon another ship slipped into an anchorage. The ship was flying the British flag and dropped anchor near the Mary Spark. Captain Amadas was informed by Mr. Berns of the new ships arrival. He immediately went out on the deck and with his spyglass; he observed the name of the ship was The Golden Hind. Every captain in the British fleet knew that ship was sailed by Francis Drake, a favorite at Queen Elizabeth's court.

Drake was the dread of the Spanish maritime. Drake had intercepted more Spanish galleons and relieved them of their treasures than any other British privateer. He was also infamous as one who raided the Spanish colonies taking their jewels and gold.

Captain Barlowe was exceptionally good friends with Drake and had originally met him several years before at court. Mr. Fernandez had sailed with him as his pilot on several missions around the Atlantic.

A jolly boat was launched with Mr. Fernandez aboard and an invitation was extended to Drake and his first officers to dine with the Captains Barlowe and Amadas, as well as Mr. Fernandez and Mr. Harriot that evening.

Later that evening and before everyone arrived, Captain Barlowe selected several of his vintage bottles of wine. Captain Amadas had the jolly boat lowered and along with Mr. Fernandez and Mr. Berns, rowed over to the Mary Spark.

Captain Barlowe had an elaborate meal prepared and delivered to his cabin just as the guests arrived. Captain Amadas knew of Captain Drake and his reputation as an explorer and adventurer, but had never had the pleasure of meeting him.

Introductions were made all around and included Thomas Harriot who was the last to join the party. Captain Amadas offered everyone a round of his vintage wine. Drake commented on the wines bouquet and the smoothness of its taste.

"Gentlemen," Drake said, "this wine is superb and it reminds me of a keg of wine I came across at the Governors Palace in Santo Domingo about a year ago. I broke open the keg, sat down at the governor's dining table and shared a glass with him and his wife. When I left that elegant company a few hours later, I relieved the governor's wife of her jewels and had my men carry the wine from their wine cellar to our waiting ship. I shared the rest of the opened keg with my crew once we were safely at sea."

"The wine that everyone is enjoying this evening was purchased in Paris when I escorted the Queen and her party as she visited the Dauphin a few years ago," Amadas said.

"So tell me," Drake inquired, "what are you gentlemen doing so far from England?"

The two captains looked at one another to determine which one would speak first. Amadas gestured to Barlowe to take the lead.

"Well sir, if you must know, we have been ordered by the Queen to go to America and locate a suitable location for a colony. In the meantime, we must construct a fort to protect us in the event we are attacked by the local natives or the Spanish. A second ship loaded with supplies is scheduled to arrive within the next few months. After we have explored and made contacts with the friendly natives, we will leave behind a few men who will occupy the fort until the third ship arrives from England with the colonists. At that point, our job will have been completed and the men from the second expedition will return home."

"Allow me to pose a simple question. Do you gentlemen really believe that an English colony will be successful in America?" Drake said with a smile in his voice.

Everyone just sat quietly and looked down to evade answering his question.

Drake took a long pause before he continued. "Gentlemen, let me assure you, based on my experience this is a very hostile land. The Spanish are struggling to hold on to their small settlement at St. Augustine. People like me, and worse, raid them a few times a year."

Drake slightly changed the subject. "The natives after a time will become hostile and refuse to trade. Eventually, everyone's morale will become depleted and they will all want to return to England. The life they attempted to escape from, in hindsight, will not look all that bad."

Drake noticed the expressions on their faces. "I don't want to discourage you gentlemen, and you must follow the directions of our Queen. But in my opinion, you are on the fools errand."

After a moment of silence, Captain Barlowe looked directly at Drake and said, "We appreciate your candid opinion and I know it's based on your experience sailing around the Americas for years. But, as you said, we have our orders and will comply to do the best of our ability to locate a suitable location for an English colony in America."

Drake raised his glass and said, "Here is to the success of your establishing a colony in the New World."

They all raised their glasses and repeated the toast.

After a pause in the conversation, Captain Amadas casually mentioned to Drake, "I have some information that may be of interest to you, sir."

Drake took a sip of his wine. "And what information might that be, sir."

"We were about to embark on a mission with the permission of the Queen that would have had us intercept a Spanish galleon sailing from Santo Domingo loaded with gold and jewels to Spain. At the last minute, Sir Walter Raleigh ordered us to sail to America instead. After this meeting, I will show you our charts, sir, where we expected to intercept that galleon. Since everything that you do on the high seas is in the interest of the Queen and county, I feel obligated to share this information with you."

Barlowe shook his head in agreement.

Drake smiled and raised his glass once more, "Gentlemen, to your patriotism." The glasses were raised and Amadas whispered, "God save the Queen."

They continued their dinner listening to Drake tell stories of his adventures sailing around the known world.

The next morning, Captains Amadas, Barlowe and pilot Fernandez met aboard the Ark Royal to discuss the final leg of their trip across the Atlantic. Fernandez estimated that according to the course he was planning, it would take about five weeks and estimated the leg to be less than sixteen hundred miles. He emphasized that it was imperative that the ships not get separated during the journey.

"If we are to establish the beginning of a colony, all the manpower we can muster is essential. In the event we encounter a storm and get separated, I have made duplicate charts of the proposed route and the anticipated landing area." Fernandez remarked.

Barlowe said that he would have his navigator go over the charts and if he had any questions, he would have him meet with Fernandez and resolve any confusion he may experience.

After the meeting, the captains agreed that they would leave the harbor on the evening tide.

As they were making preparations to leave, several more ships sailed into the harbor. Once they dropped their anchors, they launched their jolly boats and rowed over to Drakes ship, The Golden Hind.

Both the Ark Royal and the Mary Spark sent details of men to the island for the last time to fill additional casks of water and purchase some incidentals of food that they believed was going to be needed for the journey. They also purchased some items that would be used to trade with the Native Americans, such as knives, hatches, spoons, pans and clothing items.

After all the work was completed on the island and the detail was about to leave, one of the crew members from the Mary Spark, who had previously been ashore on several sojourns could not be found. It was eventually learned from one of his shipmates, that he had formed a romantic friendship with a young female Portuguese beauty and had gone into hiding. When Captain Barlowe was informed of this disobedience by one his crew he was furious. Although he didn't want to postpone sailing with the tide, he vowed that he would stop by the island on the return trip and have the man arrested for desertion and interfering with the mission.

At 1500, according to the sun dial, the tide began to retreat.

Anchors on both ships were aweigh, the sails were unfurled, and the ships began a slow traverse out of the harbor into the ocean. A course of south west was set and the mission was on its second leg.

The morale of the crew was high and everyone was anticipating reaching their destination, the coast of America and establishing a colony in the New World for the Queen and country.

Both of the captains called their crews to attention every day, gave them updates on their positions and an estimation of when they were expected to reach their destination. Five weeks was a long time to be at sea with no land in sight and if leadership wasn't careful, morale could be affected and have negative effects on the entire mission.

Once a week extra rations of food and rum were distributed to the crew. The crew was divided into two duty sections and each section took six-hour shifts, seven days a week. During the hours of darkness to dawn, two-hour watch shifts were established to keep the men that were on watch fresh and alert. Morale continued to be very high throughout.

Near the end of the fifth week around 1000 land was sighted. It stretched along the entire horizon. As they got closer, the ships began to make soundings to determine the depth of the water. When they were about a quarter of mile from the land, the captains agreed to have the Ark Royal sail north and the Mary Spark sail south looking for the inlets into the bay (Pamlico Sound) that Fernandez had noticed when he sailed with Drake previously.

Eventually, the Ark Royal came upon a cut in the land where the ocean entered the sound. Flares were set off to signal the Mary Spark that an inlet had been discovered. The Mary Spark turned north to rendezvous with the Ark Royal.

The Ark Royal lowered a jolly boat and Mr. Berns and five

crewmen rowed to the opening of the inlet. They began to take soundings throughout the entire inlet. They learned that the inlet was two fathoms deep in the center. The inlet had a seventy-five-foot width, which would just allow both of the ships, one at a time, entrance into the sound without running aground. Mr. Berns also estimated that the tide was still coming in and he had concerns that once the tide went out, the depth of the water would diminish and cause a ship at low tide to run aground. Each of the ships had a draft of six feet, five inches.

The Ark Royal waited patiently for the arrival of the Mary Spark. Once the ships were in proximity to one another, the two captains and Mr. Fernandez held a conference. It was decided to back off the shore about a half mile and drop anchor. In the meantime, they intended to send two jolly boats through the channel and search for the island that Mr. Fernandez had noticed when he had sailed along this stretch of land with Drake. It was agreed that the best position to setup the beginnings of a camp would be on that island.

The island had two advantages. First, it would provide protection from any storms that may come out of the ocean. Secondly, it would be a good place to explore from since what existed on the mainland was unknown at this time.

As the jolly boats passed though the inlet, they could see way off in the distance the island that had been spotted by Fernandez on his previous trip with Drake. They also noted a half dozen canoes moving toward them from the south. When they got within shouting distance, a native in one of one of the canoes stood up and made peaceful gestures to follow them south

Without showing any sign of aggression, Mr. Berns ordered the men in the jolly boats to have their weapons at the ready, but not to show or point them toward the natives.

The natives in the canoes signaled to the men in the jolly boats to follow them. Mr. Berns allowed natives to take the lead but continued to be cautious.

The canoes paddled, but the jolly boats used their portable sails to traverse the fifteen miles up the sound to an island the natives referred to as Croatan. (This island today is known as Cape Hatteras.)

After several hours of sailing, Berns and his men were welcomed to the Croatan village by these friendly natives. They were offered food, drink, and, through sign language, were invited to spend the night in their village. Berns was concerned that if they didn't return to the waiting ships, the captains would be concerned that something had happened to them.

Berns ordered two of the men who had accompanied him in the jolly boat to return to the ships and inform them of their location. Fortunately, the men sailing the jolly boat had a southerly wind and the tide had been ebbing to assist them back down the sound.

The Croatoans were awe-struck with these white men from across the ocean. It seemed that at some point in time, Berns assumed that Drake had visited their village and traded with these savages. Through sign language, the Croatoans described Drake and his men who had visited them in the past. And then, they produced some English items that Drake had traded.

After a few hours of sign language, it was established that the Croatoans were willing to provide them with food and other items to assure their sustenance. They further offered to allow them to camp next to their village.

When Berns informed them through clumsy sign language that they intended to set up camp on the island to the north, the Croatoans communicated to them that it could be a dangerous place to camp. The chief drew in the sand a crude map showing a large river just west of the island, and then pointed out that there were several tribes of hostile natives all along that river who would in all probability attack them.

Berns decided that he would relay this information to Captains Amadas and Barlowe and recommend for the time being they set up camp on Croatan Island.

Berns and his party left early the next morning to return to their ships and guide them up the sound.

CHAPTER III

When Berns and his jolly boat crew reached the inlet the tide was still ebbing. He had the crew row out to the Ark Royal and reported to Captain Amadas what the Croatoans told him. After a while, Amadas decided he needed to discuss the situation with Barlowe. A jolly boat was launched and, along with Berns and two crew members rowed over to the Mary Spark.

Since it was almost lunch time, Barlowe invited them into his cabin for a working lunch. Berns briefed Barlowe on the experience he had with the Croatoans the day before. He said that the Croatoans informed him that the island located in the sound is referred to as Roanoke after the natives that lived there.

The Croatoans also told him that the Roanoke natives are hostile in nature and cannot be trusted. Amadas and Barlowe considered the information helpful and they would be cautious in dealing with them.

When the working lunch was completed, Captain Amadas returned to his ship and prepared to enter the sound. Mr. Berns once again had a jolly boat launched to lead the way through the inlet. The Ark Royal took the lead followed closely by the Mary Spark and both ships made their way safely into the sound.

Once the ships were in the sound, the jolly boat turned north toward the island taking soundings to determine the depth of the water. It took more than three hours to reach their destination.

As they cautiously sailed up the east side of the island, they observed a small natural harbor at the north east side. They continued to sail around the island where they discovered a native village on the North West side. Further to the west there was what appeared to be a large river that emptied into the sound.

The natives on the shore waved to them in a friendly manner. The ships dropped their anchors, lowered a jolly boat, and rowed ashore. Mr. Berns, using sign language communicated to the Roanoke chief that they came from across the sea and were searching for a place to bring some of their people to live.

While Mr. Barns was establishing a rapport with the Roanoke, Thomas Harriot could estimate after some mathematical calculations that the island of Roanoke was approximately twenty-miles long and six-miles wide. It was also noted that the island was teeming with wild life such as deer, hares and variety of fowl. It was further noted that there was dense forest that extended all the way down to the shoreline.

Mr. Berns, after a few hours, returned to the Ark Royal and informed Captain Amadas that the Roanoke welcomed their presence.

After considering the topography of the island, it was decided that for their purposes, the inlet that was observed as they sailed up the east side of the island was the preferred site for a temporary location.

They aweigh their anchors and sailed around the rest of the island and back up the east side and into the small harbor.

Once the ships were anchored and secured, jolly boats were launched with crewmen and soldiers with their harquebuses at the ready. Once it was established that the area was free from any danger, the jolly boats began traversing back and forth from the ships unloading supplies. After everything was ashore, the captains had decided that twenty crewmen and ten soldiers would remain on the island and begin to clear a large area, as well as construct habitable living facilities and a stockade enclosure. Although the Roanokes on first contact appeared to be friendly, Mr. Berns reminded everyone of what he was told by the Croatoans and they decided to exercise caution.

As they wandered into the woods, some of the soldiers discovered that there was an abundance of berries and grapes growing nearby. One of the soldiers saw two ducks just off the shoreline. He raised his harquebus and fired killing both fowl with one shot. The other soldiers saw a flock of wild duck begin to fly at the sound of the first shot. With their harquebuses raised, they fired into the flock of fleeing birds and killed several more. There was little doubt what was going to be served for dinner that night.

As they were going about their work near the waterline, a crewman noticed the water teeming with fish. When he returned to the ship in a jolly boat, he informed the crew aboard of his observation and requested some fishing supplies.

The jolly boat was loaded with more supplies to be taken ashore and a large net to catch the fish. When he arrived back on shore, the crewman along with several of his shipmates waded into the water and spread the net. In a wide circle, they pulled the net toward the shore. The net was full of variety of fish of all sizes. Several more crewmen approached the net and began to put the captured fish into large baskets.

Captains Barlowe and Amadas came ashore about the time the fish were being scooped into the baskets and they also noticed two of the crewmen removing the feathers of the several ducks that were recently shot. Amadas suggested that a feast be prepared that evening and have everyone partake. To ensure that the ships were going to be properly manned for the night, Mr. Berns and Mr. Harris were ordered to make duty rosters.

The captains, accompanied by four soldiers, wandered deep into the woods admiring the trees that were in close proximity to the site of their proposed temporary colony. It was agreed that these trees were going to provide all the building materials that would be needed for the houses and the stockade to protect the new settlers from any attacks.

That evening in shifts, the crew and soldiers enjoyed a feast of fresh food. This was their first taste of fresh meat since leaving Porta Delgada. The rum that had been previously purchased from the Portuguese was passed out to everyone. Morale was at an all time high among the crew and soldiers.

The captains and their first mates discussed their next move. They decided to leave the Ark Royal anchored in the cove and sail the Mary Spark to the island of Croatan. They discussed that the sound could be controlled with a fort at each end. Construction was to begin the very next day on Roanoke Island. The construction of a fort at Croatan would be decided at a later time. The Mary Spark was selected to leave once the fortifications at the Roanoke site were completed and go back up the sound to explore.

Harriot was anxious to begin exploring Roanoke Island and the mainland to the west for any metal alloys that could be mined. Captain Amadas gave him permission to begin his explorations early the next morning. The captain assigned two soldiers to accompany him for protection.

Early the next morning, as construction on the new settlement was getting underway; Harriot along with two soldiers took a jolly boat and rowed around to the north end of the island to meet with the Roanoke.

When they arrived at the Roanoke village they were once again greeted with friendship. Harriot understood that the Roanokes were fascinated with the presentation of the English in their huge boats and fancy clothing. They wanted desperately to trade with the English and were anxious for their friendship.

Harriot had a natural talent for learning languages and he immediately began to develop a vocabulary of the Algonquian, which only consisted of about one hundred words. He observed that some of the Roanoke natives were wearing items made of copper.

When he questioned the chief about the copper, he was told that there was a mine about twenty miles into the mainland and promised to take him there sometime in the future. When Harriot inquired about what was up the body of water to the west, the chief said there were three Indian villages along the north side. They were Dasamonqueponke, Secotan and the Aquascogoc.

The Roanoke chief indicated that they were in hostile conflict with the Secotans. He wanted the English to join him in destroying them. Harriot refused to takes sides in the conflict.

Harriot referred to the body of water to the immediate west of the island as Roanoke (later named Albemarle Sound), and after trading some goods with the Roanoke Harriot and his two soldiers boarded the jolly boat and rowed to the mainland. They went ashore for about an hour exploring and then sailed up the Albemarle Sound a few miles when they came to the village of the Dasamonqueponke. Once again they were greeted in a friendly manner and Harriot had a long talk with the chief. He questioned him as to the location of the copper mine, but what the chief told him didn't confirm what he was told by the chief of the Roanoke. Harriot deduced that he was getting the runaround and cut short his talk. He remained at that village for the night and was given a royal feast by the Dasamonqueponke chief.

Meanwhile back at Roanoke Island, the construction was well underway, so Captains Amadas and Barlowe made the decision to send the Mary Stark back up the fifty miles of the Pamlico Sound to Croatan Island. With a skeleton crew at dawn the following day, she aweigh her anchor, unfurled the sails and began the trip up the sound. As they were sailing, they noticed another large body of water at the confluence with the Pamlico Sound (later named Pamlico River).

Although they had a good wind at their back, it took nine hours to carefully sail up the sound to reach their destination. When they were within a half-mile from the shoreline of the island, they could see a large group assembled on the shore waving at them. The group was made up of natives and crew members that Mr. Berns had left behind.

Two of the crew and two of the Croatan chiefs boarded a canoe and rowed out to the Mary Stark. Captain Barlowe greeted the visitors and welcomed them aboard the ship. One of the crew members that had accompanied them to the ship had managed to learn a little of their language in the short time he had stayed with them.

Captain Barlowe conducted a tour of the ship and the crew member, as best he could, translated the conversation between the chiefs and the captain. One of the chiefs invited the captain and the crew to come ashore that evening for a feast.

Captain Barlowe had a sixth sense and did not completely trust the Croatoans. He instructed Mr. Harris to stay aboard the ship that evening and keep a careful watch with orders not to allow any of the natives to approach the ship. Although they appeared to be friendly natives, his cautious side was telling him that they were capable of turning hostile at the least provocation.

When Captain Barlowe arrived at the village that evening, he observed that the crewmen who had been left behind by Mr. Berns had begun constructing longhouses in the native fashion. The crew members informed him that the natives had assisted in the construction as well. In addition to a longhouse that would accommodate thirty or so crew and soldiers, there was a smaller structure that was designed especially for the ships officers. The crew had even made some crude furnishings. The captain accepted the invitation of the crew to spend the night ashore.

Through the clumsy interpretation of the crewman, Barlowe queried the chief of the Croatoans about what other native tribes lived along the sound and up the two long bodies of water that emptied into the sound. He was told that on the north side of the Pamlico River there were the Acuscogoc, Cotan, and Secota. On the south side there was a people known as the Pomelock.

Barlowe learned in the course of conversation with the chief that his name was Quick Fox. Apparently, when the chief was a young boy he was very fleet footed.

After extensive questioning, Barlowe learned from the chief that there were three settlements of natives up the Albemarle Sound along the shoreline and one village on the Chowan River where the sound splits in two directions. This information corroborated the information told to Harriot when he met with the chief of the Dasamonqueponke. The chief told Barlowe that over the years the Croatoans and those tribes have been, off and on, at war with one another. He reiterated to Barlowe that it would not be safe for him and his men to establish a settlement on Roanoke Island. He urged him to settle with them on Croatan. Barlowe dismissed the chief's warning. He knew that the chief would like to keep the English close to them for trading purposes. Barlowe learned that evening that other white men had stopped over at Croatan from time to time and traded. He was pretty confident that the chief was referring to Francis Drake and his men.

Barlowe had previously learned from his conversation with Drake when they met on the Island of Sao Miguel, that there was a bay (Chesapeake) a hundred or so nautical miles to the north that may provide good land to establish a colony. When Barlowe questioned Quick Fox about this other bay, the chief told him that there were several warlike tribes that lived there and that he and his crew would most likely die if they insisted on sailing there.

"All of the land to the north is controlled by a great war chief that lives up a river [York] that empties into that bay," Quick Fox said.

For the next few days, Barlowe and his men were invited to go on hunting expeditions into the mainland. Barlowe observed an abundance of wild life in the woods and the sound was plentiful with fish.

After living with the Croatoans for several days, Barlowe conferred with his second in command, John Harris, and shared with him that he had specific orders from Raleigh to explore the Pamlico Sound. He further said that he has an obligation to explore the bay to the north to search out a good location for a colony. Raleigh wanted a detailed account of what he was to find and to put the information in a written report for him.

"Mr. Harris, prepare the Mary Stark to sail with the tide tomorrow. We will leave ten of the crewmen here to complete the structures and to learn more about the land from the Croatoans, but have the remainder of the men, including the soldiers, go aboard tonight."

"Aye sir," Mr. Harris replied. He began to round up the men and soldiers and then ferried them to the ship.

Just before dawn the next morning the tide began to ebb. The anchor was aweigh and the sails unfurled. The wind was coming out of the south and provided the fuel that moved the Mary Stark down the sound thirty miles to the inlet that emptied into the Atlantic. It took them almost four hours to reach their destination.

The inlet finally came into sight, but the Mary Stark was faced with a receding tide. Consequently, the ship had to wait until the tide reversed to make the channel passable. Barlowe estimated that it would be at least several hours before they would pass into the Atlantic.

In the meantime, a jolly boat was lowered with Barlowe and four soldiers aboard. They rowed along the strip of land that separated the sound from the ocean. There was sparse vegetation on this narrow land; however, it was teeming with fowl and turtles. The soldiers at the command of Barlowe collected the turtles and shot several wild ducks. They explored about a mile and a half more of the windswept land and then returned to the ship.

Barlowe ordered that the turtles be turned over to the cooks and requested they make a soup to be served with the roosted ducks for all aboard.

After a delicious dinner was served, Barlowe stood on the deck of the Mary Stark and observed the sun disappear over the horizon which offered a beautiful sight.

Once the night fell over the sound and the darkness closed in all around, those who didn't have the watch settled down on the deck and went to sleep.

At dawn the next morning, the crew who had been on watch called out that the tide was rising. Barlowe came on deck and observed that the tide was high enough to attempt their passage into the ocean.

Barlowe eventually gave the order to aweigh the anchor, unfurl the sails and begin moving into the channel. It only took less than ten minutes once they entered the inlet before they were experiencing the deep water of the ocean.

Back on Roanoke Island, Harriot returned to the cove where Captain Amadas was directing the construction of buildings and a stockade enclosure. Harriot shared with him his experience meeting with the Dasamonqueponke and what he had learned about the native tribes up the Albemarle Sound. He told Amadas that in his opinion they should recommend the Roanoke site for temporary settlement rather than Croatan Island. Although they had assumed that Drake had traded with them in the past, they still hadn't proved their trustworthiness. "In addition," he said, "there is much sustenance both on the Roanoke Island and in the woods of the mainland."

He had learned from the Dasamonqueponke that they were at war with the Croatoans. "If the colonists befriend the Croatoans, I fear that they will eventually get entangled in their disputes."

Harriot requested that Amadas sail with him up the sound to make contact with the native villages that he was told by the Dasamonqueponke existed there. "We should survey the land in the mainland for a possible site or sites for future colonization," he said.

Amadas listened carefully to what he had to say, but he decided that he was needed on the island to oversee the clearing and construction.

The next day, Harriot along with two soldiers in a jolly boat went back to the Roanoke village at the north end of the island.

His reasons for revisiting the village were first to continue his study of the Algonquian language, and secondly, he wanted to collect as much information about the native settlements up the sound.

Meanwhile, the Mary Stark had sailed out about a mile into the Atlantic and made a forty-five degree turn toward the north. According to Drake, once they sailed a little over a hundred miles, they would experience some turbulent water from a large river (James) that was at the confluence of a bay.

After three and a half days sailing, they reached the confluence and then they sailed on for another thirty miles until they came to the mouth of another large river York.

Sailing on for another two days and just as Drake had predicted, the Mary Stark passed another large river on the left.

Another day passed as the Mary Stark continued sailing up the bay and it was at that point both shorelines became visible. Barlowe ordered the ship to move closer to the eastern shore. When they were about a quarter of a mile from the shoreline, the anchor was dropped and a jolly boat was launched.

The jolly boat was staffed by four soldiers, four crewmen and Mr. Harris. They rowed close and parallel along the shoreline. After about a mile up the bay, they went ashore and secured the jolly boat by a line to a tree, and then the company of men began to walk the beach for another half-mile north, while observing the woods for anything that showed any signs of life.

Suddenly, one of the soldiers spotted two human forms about another half mile in front of them. One was an adult and the other appeared to be a child. They hadn't seen Mr. Harris and his party. These two individuals were intent on fishing and did not observe the soldiers and crew approaching. The small boy who was standing by the water's edge finally caught sight of the approaching group and called out to the adult who was in the water up to her waist. The soldiers moved in fast, secured the boy and before the young woman could come ashore, the soldiers were upon her.

The child was estimated to be about six or seven years of age. As a soldier was holding him tightly, the child brandished a knife and attempted to stab his assailant. The soldier disarmed him without much of an incident. The two soldiers who had waded into the water took the young woman by her arms. She struggled with them as they brought her ashore.

After the young woman and the boy were tied securely together, Mr. Harris ordered two of the crew and one of the soldiers to escort the two natives back to the Mary Stark. The young woman who appeared to be about sixteen or seventeen years of age was screaming at the top of her lungs. The soldiers readied their harquebuses and faced the woods for the possibility of an attack. Mr. Harris ordered one of the crewmen who were escorting the young woman to take a handkerchief from his head and tie it around her mouth to muffle the sound of the screams. The detail escorting the prisoners quickly turned and began to move in the direction down the beach to where the Mary Stark was anchored.

Mr. Harris and the other crewmen and soldiers moved on down the beach exploring as they traipsed along.

As the group moved along the beach and observed the water, it was noted that the fish were abundant. On several occasions, they saw a deer on the beach as they approached and there were turtles everywhere. The sightings of all this wildlife assured them that they would not be in need of sustenance.

After walking another half-mile, they noticed fresh water running across the beach, out of the woods and into the bay. They decided to follow the stream to locate its source.

After forging about a half-mile into the woods and following the fresh water to its source, they came upon a fresh water lake that seemed to extend for several miles. There was a crudely-built boat that had the appearance it had been roughly hollowed out of a log. It was resting on the bank of the lake.

After some conversation about the boat, the men came to the conclusion that it must have belonged to the young woman and her little boy companion. They further assumed that her village must be nearby. Not knowing whether or not these natives were friendly, they decided to retreat back to the bay and investigate the lake further after the young woman had been questioned.

Meanwhile, the crewmen had escorted the young woman and the boy back to the jolly boat. They decided to further ensure that the young woman could not escape while they were rowing her to the Mary Stark, so they bound her hands and ankles before placing her into the craft.

When they reached the portside of the ship, a crewman on deck lifted the child into his arms. Two additional crewmen took hold of the young woman's arms and lifted her onto the deck.

The two prisoners were offered food and water which they accepted. The crewman who had translated for Barlowe with the Croatan was brought forward to address the woman in her native language, Algonquian.

Using the little of the Algonquian language available to him, the crewman with his British accent asked, "Where is your village located?"

The young woman looked at him with some relief that he spoke her language. After a slight pause, she began to explain to him that she and her brother had been captured several weeks ago by a tribe on the eastern side of the bay. She had managed to escape two nights ago along with her little brother. She explained that the boat that she had escaped in was too heavy to drag from the lake to the bay.

The crewman asked again, "Where is your tribe's village?"

The woman pointed south west toward the western shoreline across the bay.

"What is the name of your people?" he inquired.

"My people are called the Rappahannock," she proudly announced.

Barlowe spoke up and said, "As soon as the detail of men ashore return, I intend to cross the bay and make contact with this woman's people."

An hour later, the jolly boat appeared with the remaining crew and soldiers. The anchor was aweigh and the sails were unfurled. A course was set for the western side of the bay.

The crewman stood next to the young woman and translated her directions to the helmsman. After sailing for about an hour and a half, the young woman pointed to the mouth of a large river that emptied into the bay. As the Mary Stark held a steady course the crew began to look for signs of life along its northern shore. The young woman told the crewman that her village was a few miles up from the river's mouth on the north side.

As the Mary Stark moved slowly and cautiously up the river taking continual soundings, the crew observed natives moving in and out of the tree line.

At that point, the crewman turned to the young woman and asked, "What are you called?"

With a smile, the young woman said, "I am called Hurit." Proudly she said that in her language the name means "beautiful."

The crewman decided to flatter her by saying in his floundering Algonquian, "Yes, you are."

As Hurit had stated the village was on the north side of the river. Many warriors with bows and arrows at the ready lined the shore.

Hurit waved to them and in Algonquian informed her people that these people are friends and rescued her from their enemies.

Canoes were launched and about fifty warriors rowed out to the ship. In the lead canoe was what Barlowe believed to be the chief. Barlowe estimated the population of the village to be about five hundred and possibly more. When the canoes were alongside the Mary Stark, the chief was helped aboard. Hurit informed the crewman that in addition to being the chief of the Rappahannocks, he was her father. Several more warriors climbed aboard the ship and looked around in amazement.

Captain Barlowe was introduced to the chief whose name was Pajackok. He thanked Barlowe for rescuing his daughter and returning her safely to her people.

Captain Barlowe along with his crewman translator took the group of Rappahannocks on a tour of the ship. He explained in the best terms he could muster that he was from across the sea and was searching for a place to settle some of his people along the bay.

After the tour of the Mary Stark was complete, Pajackok invited Barlowe and his crew to a feast later that evening in the village. Barlowe cautiously accepted his invitation.

Pajackok, Hurit, and the little boy left the ship and boarded one of the several canoes that had been secured to the side of the Mary Stark. They then all rowed back to the beach and entered the village. Hundreds of the Rappahannock crowded around them as they walked toward a longhouse and disappeared inside.

Barlowe requested Mr. Harris to make a list of crew and soldiers who would accompany him to the feast that evening. He wanted to ensure that a security watch was in place on the ship. Barlowe was being cautious based on his experiences traveling the world and dealing with peoples who lived in the Stone Age. He reflected upon some of the unpleasant encounters he had had during his naval career.

That afternoon was spent meeting with Mr. Harris and Fernandez to determine where they would sail next. Fernandez suggested that they go further up the river and explore its topography. Mr. Harris disagreed with Fernandez's suggestion. He believed that it would be more practical if they covered more ground by continuing up the bay to seek out more possible colony locations for the settlers when they would arrive.

"After all that is the purpose of our mission," Mr. Harris reminded them.

After much more discussion back and forth, Barlowe agreed with Mr. Harris and announced that after spending a day with the Rappahannock people, they would sail further up the bay.

That evening, Barlowe and a number of his men went ashore and were greeted with the best hospitality the Rappahannock could offer. They enjoyed a sumptuous feast of fowl and dog. There was dancing by the Rappahannock women and after a while they entertained many of the crewmembers individually. Barlowe was offered to be entertained by one of the more beautiful maidens of the village but he politely refused.

Barlowe sat down with the chiefs of the tribe in a longhouse, smoked the pipe of peace and friendship and then learned as much as he could. He was interested in what was up at the head of the bay.

Through his crewman translator, Barlowe learned from Pajackok that he would encounter several hostile tribes who had encountered white men in the past and considered them enemies. Barlowe knew immediately that he was referring to the Spanish expeditions of the bay years before. Barlowe had spent time in Spain in the mid-1570s as a young man and heard tales of the Spanish Navy exploring the lands up and down the east coast of America. He was told by his Spanish teachers that the purpose of these expeditions was to expose the natives of America to the true religion and convert them. Barlowe was told by one of his professors, when he was attending the university in Seville, that a few years before, two missionaries were taken up to a bay in America and left on its shores to make contact and convert the natives. When the Spanish returned two years later, the missionaries had disappeared without a trace.

The Spanish assumed that the natives had killed them. So, and without asking any questions, the Spanish killed every native they came across in the upper bay region, whether or not they had been involved in the killing of the missionaries. "Needless to say, those natives have long memories and consider all white men their enemy. That was a big mistake made by my people," the professor told Barlowe.

Once again, Barlowe thought to himself, *the Spaniards have poisoned the native peoples of this land with their fanatic religious beliefs.*

After he smoked the peace pipe with Pajackok, he had Mr. Harris round up the crew members who had wandered off in the night with the native maidens. After all the crew was accounted for they were ordered back aboard the Mary Stark.

Early the next morning, Barlowe had a cannon fired to salute the Rappahannock and once the anchor was aweigh and the sails unfurled, he decided to take Fernandez's recommendation and slowly sail up the river. After they sailed about ten miles, the river began to narrow and become shallower. For fear of becoming grounded, he had the helmsmen turn the ship around and sailed back down the river.

As he passed the Rappahannock village, he once again had a cannon fired and waved to the natives on the beach as they went by. They continued slowly down the river and out into the bay. After they reached a quarter mile out, the helmsman turned the ship north up the bay.

In the early afternoon several of the crew became ill. They began to have bouts of diarrhea and vomiting. At first, the crewman aboard who served as a medic diagnosed their symptoms as food poisoning. As time passed, several more crew and soldiers came down with this mysterious malady. They began to suspect that the illness may be more than food poisoning.

Barlowe began to show signs of the mysterious illness and eventually was bedridden. Mr. Harris took command of the Mary Stark as she continued sailing up the bay. They passed several rivers emptying into the bay on both the east and west sides, and by the time they had traveled seventy miles up the bay from the Rappahannock River only Mr. Harris and three of the crew were not inflicted with the illness. The remainder of the crew and soldiers were too weak from their symptoms to perform their duties.

Sailing the ship farther and taking care of the sick, it became too much of a task for the three crew members and Mr. Harris. After discussing the situation with Captain Barlowe, it was mutually decided to find a safe harbor and drop anchor.

Such a harbor was finally identified on the left side of the bay and the Mary Stark sailed directly into it. They passed several small islands as the ship moved slowly stopping periodically and taking soundings. After a few miles the shorelines closed in and there was land about a half-mile directly in front of the ship. (Later the site of Fort McHenry)

Mr. Harris ordered the anchor to be dropped and with his spyglass surveyed the land in all directions.

Early the next morning, the crewman watch spotted several canoes heading directly towards them. He awakened Mr. Harris and the other crew members from their sleep. The all took up arms. Natives in the canoes began showing signs of hostility by waving spears and pointing them at the ship. Mr. Harris went into immediate action. The last thing that he wanted to do was to communicate to these screaming warriors that the majority of the crew aboard the ship were incapacitated.

He called every crewman and soldier who had the ability to stand and hold a harquebus to the ships rail and point their weapons at the oncoming flotilla.

Mr. Harris and the three well crewmen took aim at these natives and when they were in range gave the order to open fire. Several of these warriors fell out of or into their canoes either dead or wounded. At that point, the entire flotilla turned and began paddling toward the shoreline. Once they reached the beach, they disembarked from their canoes and ran up and down the shoreline shooting arrows at the anchored ship. Their arrows fell several yards short of their intended targets.

Under the circumstances, Mr. Harris took an assessment of the situation and asked several of the sick if they were well enough to stand watch. Two soldiers and four crewmen volunteered. Mr. Harris knew that they could not stay at anchorage more than a day or two.

After a while, he conferred with the captain and informed him of the situation. The captain advised that as soon as possible they should aweigh the anchor, unfurl the sails and head back down the bay.

During the night several attempts were made by the hostile natives to get closer to the Mary Stark and they fired their arrows at the men standing watch. As a result of their aggression several more warriors were shot.

At dawn the next morning, the bodies of the natives who had been shot the night before were floating in the water not far from the ship. It had been a stressful night at the watch. Mr. Harris called for the anchor to be aweigh and the sails unfurled as the 'Mary Stark' slowly sailed out of the harbor and into the bay. A course was set south and back toward the Atlantic Ocean.

As they passed the mouth of the Rappahannock, Captain Barlowe decided to sail back up the river to impose on their native friends and to spend some time convalescing. When they finally reached the Rappahannock Village, Mr. Harris went ashore with the crewman translator who had been one of the fortunate ones not to come down with the malady. Through the translator, he explained the situation to Pajackok who went into action immediately. Several maidens loaded down with medicinal herbs, rowed out in their canoes and began to treat the sick.

Within a day, the majority of the crew was showing signs of being cured. Barlowe was amazed at the power of the native medicine. He decided to take samples of it back to England when he returned.

After several more days of convalescing, it was decided that they had overstayed their welcome and they also wanted to return to Roanoke and meet up with Amadas.

After an evening of feasting and thanking the Rappahannock for their care and generosity, they aweigh anchor early the next morning and sailed down the river to the bay.

They had a good north wind and made good time and distance. When they reached the mouth of the bay three days later, natives were observed along the eastern side of the shoreline waving at them and requesting that they come ashore. Barlowe and his crew waved back but ignored their request and continued to sail on.

As they sailed into the ocean they maintained a southerly course until they reached the Outer Banks. Several more miles under sail and they reached the inlet that allowed them entrance to the Pamlico Sound.

Once safely through the inlet, they turned in the direction of Roanoke Island. An hour later, the island came into view and as they sailed around the east side, the mask of the Ark Royal could be seen in the distance. They entered the little harbor as they fired one of their cannons to alert their comrades.

When the Mary Stark dropped anchor about a quarter mile from the beach, Captain Amadas was observed standing on the shoreline waving to them. A jolly boat was launched with Captain Barlowe (now completely recovered from his malady) along with Mr. Harris and four crewmen all rowed ashore.

The two captains hugged each other in a friendly greeting. Captain Amadas invited the Mary Stark crew to have refreshments in one of the newly constructed houses. Captain Barlowe congratulated Amadas on the incredible progress that had been made since he was there last.

After they sat down and refreshments were served, Captain Amadas told of making contact with several natives from up the Albemarle Sound.

"They appear to be very friendly and they indicated they were interested in our trading with them," Amadas said with a tinge of doubt in his voice.

Barlowe said, "We made friends with a native tribe up the bay as well. On our return, they nursed many of us back to health with their herbs. These herbs had a magical effect. I brought some back to have them examined once we return to England."

Amadas elaborated his story about the natives he had contact with. "They invited us to come up the river to their village when we have time and trade with them. I can't leave here right now, but maybe you would like to sail up the bay, trade with them and see if you can identify any good locations for a colony."

Amadas stated that once the settlers arrived, it would be advantageous to have good relations with the local natives.

After a few more glasses of ale, Barlowe shared with Amadas his experiences traveling the upper bay. He told Amadas that in his opinion and what he observed, a settlement somewhere along the bay off of one of its many rivers would make more sense than to settle on this island.

"The way I see it, this island is a good stopping off point, but, we really have to explore the mainland for a location. From what I have observed, there are a lot of natural resources available there," Amadas said.

"My only concern with establishing any kind of settlement here, permanent or temporary is its exposure to the Spanish. As you know, they sail this stretch of the Atlantic on a regular basis," he said with a deep concern

Amadas told Barlowe that he believed his work was nearly complete on Roanoke Island and he intended to return to England before the winter set in. Barlowe said that he would take his advice and sail up the Albemarle Sound before setting sail for England as well.

Barlowe passed on his confrontation with natives seventy miles up the bay. He emphasized that it was a natural harbor and should be explored at a later date. He also mentioned the natives that appeared to be friendly at the mouth of the bay on the return voyage.

Barlow said that he wanted to give his crew a few days to rest and continue to recuperate from their illness before sailing up the Albemarle Sound. Amadas informed Barlowe that he intended to leave three soldiers on the island site to watch over the facilities after he sails.

The captains spent the rest of the day exchanging pleasantries and drinking wine.

CHAPTER IV

Three days hence, the captains shook hands and wished each other well. Captain Amadas would be on his way back to England by the time Barlowe returned from his sail up the Albemarle Sound.

Amadas selected three soldiers who had proved to be good carpenters when they weren't guarding. They were instructed to continue putting the finishing touches on the facilities that had already been constructed.

Captain Amadas aweigh anchor of the Ark Royal and began his sail up the Sound toward Croatan Island. About halfway toward their destination, they dropped anchor when they noticed a herd of deer at the shoreline. He had the crew lower a jolly boat on the portside of the ship to prevent the deer from seeing their movement and being scared away.

The crew positioned their jolly boat with the light of the setting sun at their backs, and they kept low in the boat as they slowly paddled their boat with their hands, keeping the harquebus pointed directly at the unsuspecting deer.

As the jolly boat approached the shoreline, the crewman in the front of the boat with a harquebus fired one shot into the herd. Two of the deer fell where they had been standing. The jolly boat crew pulled out the oars and rowed quickly to shore. One of the deer was still alive, but a crewman finished it off with his knife.

The deer were gutted and butchered on the spot. The meat was put into bags and transported back to the ship.

Captain Amadas decided to remain at anchor for the night and have the cook prepare the meat and serve it to the crew.

Early the next morning, the Ark Royal aweigh anchor, unfurled its sails and continued up the Pamlico Sound.

They reached Croatan Island around noon and were greeted by several Croatoans, the few soldiers and crewmen who had been left behind.

Amadas congratulated the crewmen and soldiers for their hard work in constructing living facilities on the island. He was told by a young officer who had been left behind that more than half of the Croatoans had abandoned the island and had moved to the mainland. He said that due to the drought the game was practically non-existent. He also said that growing crops was out of the question.

Meanwhile, Captain Barlowe set a course up the Albemarle Sound. Harriot sailed with Barlowe to act as a translator with any natives they would encounter. They sailed around Roanoke Island; they crossed to the left of it and turned into the mouth of Albemarle.

As he sailed about a mile into the sound, he was overtaken with what he saw. He made a comment in his diary: "Its goodly woods are full of deer, rabbits, hares and fowl in incredible abundance, not to mention the highest, reddest cedars in the world."

After a distance of about ten miles, he was greeted by three canoes of natives making friendly gestures. Harriot had previously visited their village and had assured them he would return to trade. They sailed on until the village came into sight around a bend.

Captain Barlowe had the sails lowered and the anchor dropped.

Canoes came out to the ship and several of the warriors and maidens climbed aboard. The crew greeted them as they wandered around the deck and eventually items were exchanged. One very masculine individual introduced himself as the chief and Captain Barlowe invited him to join him in his cabin. Harriot followed behind the two to do his translation duties.

In the cabin, Barlowe learned that the name of the chief was Wingina. After questioning him in his native tongue, Harriot told Barlowe that Wingina was the chief and ruled over all of the tribes up the river. He told Barlowe through Harriot that all those tribes pay tribute to him, annually. He further said that any trading with the other tribes must be approved by him. Barlowe didn't take kindly to this announcement, but he kept his temper in check.

Wingina invited the captain and his crew to a feast that evening in the village. Barlowe was reluctant to accept this invitation, but at the same time he didn't want to insult him. He accepted the invitation.

Barlowe had noticed that Wingina was limping when he walked to the cabin for their meeting.

He learned later from Harriot: "I was told by one of his warriors that he was wounded in a battle with a tribe called the Piemacum that live along the Neuse River."

That evening, Barlowe along with Harriot, several soldiers and crewmembers rowed over to the village. Before they sat down to the feast, Wingina requested a meeting with Barlowe. Barlowe, Harriot and Wingina retired to one of the longhouses and sat on a blanket. Wingina began by informing Barlowe if he wished to trade and be friends with the confederacy, they would be required to join him in war with his enemies. The last thing that Barlowe wanted to do was to commit the English to a war with any of the surrounding tribes.

"I will take your request to join you in war and discuss this matter with my superiors. I will let you know their decision before I return to England," Barlowe informed him.

"I will allow you to continue traveling up the river and visiting my people there. But, if you don't agree to assist me with my war, those villages will not be available to you in the future," Wingina said in a very determined tone.

Barlowe had Harriot question Wingina about the tribes that lived further up the river. Wingina acknowledged that there were two more villages miles up the river and lived on the opposite side from where his village was located. He refused to say, one way or the other, whether or not the Englishmen would meet with any hostility. Barlowe took from his silence on the subject that he didn't particularly want them to continue up the river and make contact with those peoples. He wanted to ensure that any and all trade would go through him.

Finally, the talks ended and they all rose from the blanket. They walked outside and joined in the feast that the soldiers and crewmen had already been enjoying.

Barlowe was troubled with Wingina's demands and attitude. He knew that Raleigh would never agree to assist one native tribe against another. One of Barlowe's and Amadas' main directives from Raleigh was to establish peaceful relations with all the native tribes. They were, however, allowed to take a defensive action when they were subject to any aggression by the natives.

After spending a day with Wingina and the Dasamonqueponke people trading trinkets for fresh food, the Mary Stark continued up the river for another twenty-five miles until they were confronted with several canoes of braves rowing toward them. Barlowe and his men made peaceful signs and allowed the natives to come alongside the ship.

Three of the warriors were allowed to board the ship and were greeted by Harriot in the Algonquian tongue. The natives were curious about the size of the Mary Stark and requested to be shown around. Barlowe told Harriot to show them the cannons and impress upon them the kind of damage only one cannon could do if fired. Harriot had the crew prepare one of the cannons for firing and had it discharged. The natives aboard witnessing the destruction the one cannon ball could do were very impressed.

This tribe was known as the Secotan and after further conversation with these natives, it was learned that what Wingina had told them was in fact true. They were required to pay tribute to him. They had received word from Wingina that they were not to trade with the English.

After a lengthy conversation with the natives aboard the ship, Barlowe learned that a few years ago the Secotan had entered into a long and bloody war with the Dasamonqueponke and after losing many braves they were forced to surrender. There were still bitter feelings among many within the tribe and Barlowe determined that one day another battle between these two native groups would reignite.

One of the visiting natives identified himself as the chief of the Secotan. His name was Pomeiooc. He insinuated to Barlowe that he would trade with the English as long as Wingina was not made aware of it.

Barlowe was tempted to trade with them, but he weighed the alternatives and decided not to on this trip. *Maybe another time*, he thought. Barlowe knew that these people were suffering from a year-long drought, their crops had failed he was told, and the hunting of game was practically non-existent.

Harriot questioned Pomeiooc as to how far up the river was the next village. Pomeiooc indicated using the sun as a reference that it was another half-day sail.

Early the next morning, the Mary Stark continued her sail up the Albemarle Sound. As they sailed on the river became narrower. There were trees growing along and in the river that drew Barlowe's attention. He had the anchor dropped and a jolly boat lowered. With two crewmen they rowed ashore.

As Barlowe walked along the edge of the river, he began to inspect these curious trees. One of the crewmen with him recognized the leaves and informed Barlowe that he believed they were sassafras. Barlowe knew that if indeed these leaves were sassafras, it was like finding pound notes growing along the river.

During this time in Europe sassafras was in great demand.

When Columbus visited the New World his crew had cohabited with the natives on the Island of Hispaniola. As a result of this cohabitation, a new disease was brought back to Spain and it spread rapidly throughout the rest of Europe in a short period of time. This disease became known as syphilis. In the fifteenth century sassafras was believed to be a cure for this ravaging plight.

Barlowe had a crewman row back to the ship and collect as many bags as he could locate on the ship and return them to him on the shore.

When the crewman returned, Barlowe and the two crewmen began to fill the bags with the suspected sassafras leaves. After an hour of relinquishing the sassafras trees of their precious leaves, the crewmen and Barlowe returned to the ship.

Barlowe knew he had discovered something that was as valuable as gold. If these leaves were in fact sassafras, Raleigh could begin immediately to see a return on his investment in establishing a colony in America.

As they sailed on the river it became narrower. Directly to their front was land. On either side of this land were two rivers emptying into the sound. One river came out of the north and the other from the west (the Chowan River).

Barlow saw a village on the north side of the sound. The natives were standing on the shoreline and making peaceful signs waving to the ship. Barlowe had a jolly boat launched and rowed toward these friendly natives. He soon learned from conversing with their chief that these people were in worse shape than the last village he had passed. The drought had severely affected their growing of crops and the game had all but disappeared from the surrounding woods.

In a friendly gesture, Barlowe decided to share some of the supplies he had aboard the ship with these starving people. These people believed that the Mary Stark was sent to them by one of the gods they had been praying to for the past several months.

After meeting with some of the elders of the tribe, Barlowe explored the possibility of the tribe allowing some of the English colonists establish themselves across the river from their village.

Barlowe was thinking ahead. If the leaves that he had collected a few miles down the river were in fact sassafras, this would be an ideal location to collect, grow and export this valuable commodity.

Within a few hours of speaking with the elders of the tribe, Barlowe, Harris and Harriot boarded a jolly boat and rowed the half-mile over to the opposite shore. This site in Barlowe's opinion was located in a prime and strategic area. It looked directly down Albemarle Sound. (Today it is the site of Edenton, NC.)

He deduced that if a fort were to be built on this spot, it would have the full advantage of controlling the entire sound.

He also noted that the land appeared to be fertile although the drought had had its effect. Barlowe was going to recommend that the future colony be spread out along Albemarle Sound rather than on Roanoke Island, as some had suggested.

There were several reasons for this recommendation. First, Roanoke Island was exposed to the ocean where it could be seen by Spanish ships sailing along the coast. Secondly, this site would offer protection from the harsh Atlantic storms that were known to attack the coast without warning. And finally, they could depend on friendly natives who lived just across the river to teach them how to hunt and grow crops on the land.

When the brief tour of the site was complete, Barlowe rowed back to the ship and the Mary Stark began her sail back down the sound.

As they passed the Secotan's village, many of the warriors along the bank made threatening gestures. Barlowe had known that the Secotan weren't happy with his refusing their offer to trade. However, he believed at the present; it was more important to follow the directive of Wingina and not trade. He didn't want to experience his wrath at a later time.

Twenty-five miles further down the river, the Dasamonqueponke village came back into view. The tribe crowded the shoreline and gestured for them to come ashore. Barlowe wanted to demonstrate the power of the English and he fired a blank cannon. The Mary Stark continued on down the sound and made a short stop at Roanoke Island.

They spent a couple of hours with the few men that had been left on the island to watch over the recently constructed facilities. These men were still putting the finishing touches on the buildings.

Since it was getting dark, it was decided to spend the night on the island and continue their sail the next morning. Barlowe had supplies brought over from the ship and they dined with the island's caretakers.

Early the next morning, Barlowe wished the remaining men good luck. He took some letters that two of them had written to relatives in England and promised that he would deliver them. He had the anchor aweigh, the sails unfurled and began their trek south up the Pamlico Sound.

When they were about ten miles from Croatan Island one of the Mary Stark crew saw some Croatoans waving to them on the shoreline. Barlowe had the anchor dropped and a jolly boat launched. Barlowe, Harriot, and two crew members rowed ashore to meet with theses natives.

They informed Barlowe through Harriot that most of their people had abandoned the island and were resettling on the peninsula along the sound. The island couldn't support their people due to the drought and water was practically non-existent. As a result of the lack of water, the game had moved into the mainland.

Barlowe inquired about Captain Amadas. The Croatoans told him that Amadas had left several days ago and had taken most of the English that were on the island with him. He also took with him Manteo, a Croatoan, and Wanchese, a Secotan, back across the sea.

Barlowe and his men shared a meal with the Croatoans and spent several hours looking over the terrain before returning to the ship. Since it was getting dark, Barlowe decided to wait until morning before continuing the sail up the sound.

Late the next morning as the Mary Stark approached the island of Croatan there was people on the beach waving to them. The ship dropped anchor, lowered a jolly boat and rowed ashore.

The first to greet them were the two English left behind at their request. One was a soldier and the other a crewman from the Ark Royal. They had taken Croatoan wives and were preparing to move to the mainland with the remaining Croatoans.

Barlowe gave them some supplies from the ship and asked them to act as ambassadors while living among the Croatoans. "It's important," he said, "that the English continue to sustain good relations with these people." He wished them well, returned to the ship and prepared to sail back to England.

When Harriot had learned that Amadas had taken with him Manteo and Wanchese, he could hardly wait to return to England. He was determined to spend a considerable amount of time with them to refine his knowledge of the Algonquian language. He further had an ambition to develop a written form of that language.

As the Mary Stark aweigh its anchor, Barlowe felt a sense of accomplishment about this voyage. Its purpose was to locate a site or sites for a colony, establish good relations with the natives, and to search for economic potentials. In his opinion, all of those goals had been accomplished. He knew that when he presented the sassafras to Raleigh that he would be secure in the fact that a colony in America would be financially productive.

The Mary Stark after a day of sailing reached the inlet to the Atlantic and the tide was high. The ship eased her way through and out into the Atlantic. The weather was cooperating and for all practical purposes the seas were relatively calm. They set a course for the island of Sao Miguel and the port of Delgada.

Barlowe's reasons for wanting to stop over on the island were two fold. First, the ship would need to replenish its water supply. Secondly, he was intent on taking into custody the crewman who had gone off with a local young woman.

After three weeks at sea, the island came into view and the Mary Stark slipped into an anchorage at Delgada.

As customary, a delegation rowed out and boarded the Mary

Stark. They questioned Barlowe as to his business on the island and how long he intended to remain. Barlowe answered the questions to their satisfaction and he mentioned that they were intent on capturing the crewman who had deserted when they were last at anchor there. The delegation told Barlowe that they would not interfere with him searching for the crewman, but they would not assist in the search.

After the delegation left the ship, Barlowe had Mr. Harris form a shore detail under his command. Comprising the detail were four soldiers, four crewmen and Harriot to act as translator since he was fluent in Portuguese. The crewmen were to proceed to the fresh water source and fill twenty kegs. The soldiers were to go on a manhunt for the deserting crewman.

When the two jolly boats reached the shoreline and the detail divided in its two intended directions, Harriot immediately began his questioning of the workers at the kiosks that lined the streets of the small city. After an hour spent questioning, they were able to collect enough information that would put them on the trail of the deserting crewman and possibly arrest him.

One young woman, who identified herself as the sister of the woman who had taken a romantic interest in the missing crewman, began to volunteer some valuable information.

"I know where they are hiding," she told Harriot. "When they saw your ship come into the harbor they left for the mountains. If you'll give me some silver, I will take you to where they may be found."

When the woman's demand for silver was translated, one of the soldiers grabbed the young woman by her blouse and had Harriot translate. "You will take us there immediately if you value your life. Otherwise, I will have two soldiers take you back to our ship and you'll be tried in England for harboring a criminal which could result in a death sentence."

What the women didn't know was that the government of Sao Miguel would not permit the English to take one of their citizens to England without their permission. However, it had its effect on the young woman and it put the fear of god in her. So, she decided to cooperate regardless of a reward.

The young woman clarified her previous statement as to her relationship to the woman with the crewman. She said the woman was her stepsister and was not a blood relation. Therefore, she didn't feel an obligation to protect her.

She said that the crewman and her step-sister were hiding in a family house about an hour away in the mountains. She agreed to lead them there.

Meanwhile, the water detail along with several locals agreed to assist the crewmen with carrying the water back to the beach for a price. When they got all of the twenty kegs to the beach, they began to load two kegs at a time into the jolly boat and row them out to the ship. After ten trips all the water kegs were loaded onto the deck of the ship.

The soldiers followed the woman about five miles into the mountains. They finally came upon some cleared land where several small buildings and a stone house were located. She identified the house as one that belonged to her uncle who had temporarily moved into the city to operate his kiosk and sell his produce.

The soldiers tied the young woman to a tree and silently surrounded the house. After doing some reconnaissance, they learned that there were not any doors or windows in the rear of the house. They took up positions on each side of the house and called to the crewman to come out with his hands raised. There wasn't any response from the inside.

One of the soldiers shouted that if they didn't come out, they intended to set fire to the house.

Seconds later, the door slowly opened and the crewman, Donald Nelson, stepped out with his hands raised. Within seconds the soldiers had Nelson in chains. Nelson pleaded with the soldiers not to arrest his female accomplice. He stated to the soldiers that he had forced her to be with him. The soldiers knew that he was lying, but they didn't have any jurisdiction over her anyway.

After a brief conversation they decided to release her.

When they arrived back at the ship, Nelson was chained below deck. After a few hours and passing out rations to the crew, the Mary Stark slipped quietly out of the harbor. They now began their final leg of the voyage back to England.

Before they had left for America, Barlowe and Amadas were told by Raleigh that when they returned, to sail to the Plymouth harbor rather than their port of departure, Portsmouth. Raleigh had intended to be at Plymouth on pressing business issues. He was going to be preparing ships there for a second voyage that he intended to command.

The Mary Stark encountered a late summer storm that pushed her miles off course. As a result, it took two weeks off their expected arrival time.

Finally, the shoreline of England came into view. They located Plymouth Harbor and sailed into an anchorage. A short distance away was anchored the Ark Royal. The crewman working its decks waved enthusiastically at the crew of the Mary Stark and welcomed them home.

Barlowe was anxious to meet with Raleigh and to give him a verbal report. He was especially interested in showing him the sassafras that he discovered up the Albemarle Sound. He also knew that Raleigh would have something positive about the voyage that he could report to the Queen.

Barlowe took a small bag of the sassafras leaves, boarded a jolly boat and rowed ashore. As he was reaching the pier that jetted out into the harbor, he noticed a man standing at its edge. As he got closer, he recognized it was Raleigh.

As he stepped onto the pier, Raleigh embraced and welcomed him home. Barlowe opened the bag he was holding and requested Raleigh to peer inside. He whispered in Raleigh's ear, "Sassafras." Raleigh was ecstatic with glee at the sound of the word.

As they walked toward an inn to get some refreshment, Raleigh said that he wanted both Barlowe and Amadas to come to court within the week and meet with the Queen. "I want you and Captain Amadas to get the full credit for conducting a voyage well done."

Raleigh requested Barlowe to write a full report of his findings in America. He said as they spoke Amadas was doing likewise. The written report was to be given to Hakluyt. He was one of the Queen's close advisors and historian and the reports would be shared with the many other advisers of the Queen as well.

Later that day, Raleigh dined with Amadas and Barlowe and during that dinner informed them that the Queen had approved a second trip to America. "Only this time," he said, "there will be five ships and two 'pinnaces that would carry six hundred colonists."

In the meantime, the two natives that had returned with Amadas-Manteo and Wanchese-had taken up residence at Durham House, a mansion on the Thames River granted to Raleigh by the Queen the year before. Harriot was invited to stay there as well. He was to study with and teach the two Native Americans each other's languages.

In addition to spending time at court, Raleigh spent most of his time raising money to support a large-scale colonizing effort at Roanoke.

That December in London, Manteo and Wanchese were presented to the Queen at court.

On January 6, 1585, Raleigh was knighted during the celebration of the Twelfth Night of Christmas; shortly afterward, he assumed the title, Lord Governor of Virginia which revealed a new name for the Queen's colony.

The Virginia settlement was to be part of a larger strategy by Elizabeth in her war against Spain. She planned to send an army to the Netherlands to fight on behalf of the Protestants there, send Francis Drake to the West Indies to disrupt Spanish shipping, and also have Raleigh colonize Roanoke Island to establish a harbor for English privateers who would prey upon the Spanish.

Elizabeth made a decision not to share the fact that sassafras had been discovered in America with her advisors. It was going to be a closely guarded secret between, Raleigh, Barlowe and herself. She let it be known that she was "hopeful" that gold and silver would be found as well and that the Native Americans would be converted to Protestantism.

"And if anyone is capable of doing all this," the Queen said, "it is Sir Walter Raleigh."

CHAPTER V

Shortly after the Mary Stark arrived at Plymouth Harbor two specific events occurred. First, crewman Donald Nelson was tried for desertion before an admiralty court and sentenced to fifty lashes. The two ships, the Mary Stark and the Ark Royal were pulled into drydock to be refurbished.

In early January 1585, Raleigh began planning the second English voyage to America. He intended to head up the expedition personally, but the Queen had other thoughts. She foresaw a war with Spain in the near future and she wanted to have Raleigh by her side. There was no convincing the Queen once she had made up her mind.

Raleigh moved ahead with the plans to organize the second voyage. He chose his cousin Sir Richard Grenville to take his place. Since it was all but certain that a war between England and Spain would develop, Grenville was given a military mission as well. In addition to colonizing Roanoke for English privateers, his mission included disrupting Spanish shipping in the West Indies.

In early April, the Ark Royal and the Mary Stark were launched and joined the Lion, the Tiger and the Primrose at anchor. These ships were joined by two 'pinnaces' that were intended for exploration of the various rivers on the mainland.

Raleigh had gathered a second fleet of ships that were intended to carry supplies to the colony a few months after Grenville departed under the command of Sir Bernard Drake and were at anchor in Portsmouth Harbor

Sir Richard Grenville, often an arrogant and bullheaded man, led the fleet in his ship the Tiger and set sail in mid-April 1585. His ship was piloted by the ever-present Simon Fernandez. Colonel Ralph Lane, the recent sheriff of County Kerry, Ireland, was captain of the Primrose and was second in command. Amadas and Barlowe were in command of the Ark Royal and the Mary Spark, respectively. John White, Thomas Harriot, Manteo, and Wanchese were also aboard the various ships.

About half the colonists aboard the ships were soldiers, but there were also carpenters, farmers, cooks, shoemakers, tailors and at least one minister. All the colonists on this voyage were men.

In early May, the fleet encountered a huge ocean storm and the ships were separated. On May 11, Grenville and the Tiger stopped for a few weeks at the mosquito-ridden Mosquetal in present-day Puerto Rico to wait for the other ships that had been separated during the storm. He also spent some time repairing the damage the storm had done to the Tiger.

John White found the flora and fauna fascinating and beautiful. He spent much of his time there painting beautiful scenes.

All of the ships eventually rendezvoused with Grenville except the Primrose. If this ship didn't eventually arrive, it could put the expedition in jeopardy since it was carrying a large amount of supplies.

Grenville didn't want to wait any longer, so on June 2,[1] the Tiger, the three other ships, and pinnaces left Puerto Rico for the American coast. On June 26,[1] the fleet dropped anchor at the Outer Banks barrier island of Wococon about eighty miles to the southwest of Roanoke.

Fernandez did not fully appreciate just how treacherous navigation was in this area. Three days later, he ran the Tiger aground attempting to steer through an inlet. As a result of this oversight much of the supplies the Tiger was carrying were ruined. Grenville had planned to have an enough supplies to feed the colonists for a year. Now with this accident and the absence of the Primrose, Grenville now only had enough food for twenty days. These unanticipated dilemmas would prove critical in the coming days as he and his men interacted with the Native Americans.

When word reached the various tribes of Grenville's arrival, they were divided about how they should react toward the English. The Croatoans stood firm in their friendship. However, it was a different situation with the tribes that Wingina ruled.

Manteo left the Tiger to visit his mother who had moved with many of the Croatoans to the mainland. Grenville wanted the Croatoans to know that he intended to tour the Pamlico River and pay his respects to the tribes whose villages were located along the shoreline up that body of water. He toured the Secotan villages of Pomeiock, Aquascogoc and Secota while identifying other villages around the shores of Pamlico River.

Grenville's company of soldiers presented an impressive military force to the Secotan. John White accompanied Grenville on this tour and he made sketches of the various Native Americans and painted pictures of their villages.

Grenville knew that if he was to stay longer than the twenty days that the supplies would allow, he was going to have to impose on the native tribes for sustenance. A shortage of food among the Native Americans apparently occurred each year after a long winter and before the first harvest. This year, however, was direr due to the drought.

Grenville's need for food supplies and the drought was inevitably going to create a conflict between the English and the Secotan. In addition and to make matters worse during the absence of the English, Wingina's people had observed a total eclipse of the sun and immediately upon the colonist's reappearance a comet had slowly blazed across the sky.

Many of these Algonquians believed these to be potentially significant signs. And shortly after the English left many villages began to suffer from a quick-moving, often fatal illness such as small-pox, they saw all of these events as related.

After the tour of the Pamlico River, Grenville returned to Wococon and oversaw the repairs on the Tiger. At first, Grenville was going to leave a complement of soldiers on Wococon and continue down the seaboard until he found another inlet to cross into Pamlico Sound and then sail to Roanoke Island. However, after giving it more thought and since there was little chance to grow crops, he decided to take the entire company to Roanoke.

When Grenville finally reached Roanoke Island, he searched for the three soldiers that had been left there by Amadas to put the finishing touches on the previously built buildings. The facilities were in relatively good shape, but the men had disappeared without a trace.

It was also discovered that the Roanoke Village on the North West side of the island was deserted. The Croatoans believed that the Roanoke had moved north to form an alliance with the Powhatans and were possibly responsible for the disappearance of the soldiers.

Grenville was anxious to go privateering Spanish ships to offset the cost of the expedition. He would then return to England for more men and, supplies and then return. He placed Ralph Lane in charge of the little colony on Roanoke with a contingency of 107 men.

The Mary Stark along with two pinnaces were left for the purpose of exploring, trading with the natives, and to escape the island if necessary. Captain Amadas prepared to sail with Grenville, but at the last minute he was ordered to sail up the Chesapeake Bay and establish relations with natives along its shoreline. Amadas was expected to rendezvous with Grenville a month later in the Atlantic Spanish shipping lanes. Grenville expected to return to America by August 1586, if all went well.

Harriot stayed behind with Lane as a translator. Manteo and his companion Towaye sailed with Grenville.

Lane immediately made plans to explore the Albemarle Sound along with John White and Thomas Harriot. Barlowe had already been to its head and outlined to Lane what he would find along the way. Lane placed Barlowe in charge of the Roanoke settlement in his absence.

The Native American, Wanchese, who had spent several months in London as a guest of the English, disappeared from the settlement shortly after he arrived there.

Wanchese arrived at the village of Dasamonqueponke and had a conference with Wingina. He told him that the English could not be trusted. He further told Wingina that Grenville had visited villages of the Pomeiooc and the home of Wingina's rival and enemy, Piemacum, Aquascogoc, and finally, Secotan. Wanchese described how the English burned the village of Aquascogoc over the supposed thievery of a missing cup.

Lane was not made aware of the discovery of sassafras the year before by Barlowe. He was pretty confident that Lane would not recognize the leaf for what it was when he saw the trees along the bank of the river. He had been sworn to secrecy by Raleigh. He was confident, however, that Raleigh would inform those who had a need to know eventually.

With the information Wanchese had passed along to Wingina, he began to formulate a plan to kill the English on the island of Roanoke when the right time presented itself.

Lane had been informed by Grenville before he left that five ships loaded with supplies would arrive within the next month under the guidance of Sir Bernard Drake.

What Grenville didn't know was that at the last minute, and when they were about to leave for America, the Queen ordered Drake to sail to the Netherlands and warn the English fishing ships to be aware of Spanish war ships in the area. This diversion prevented the much needed supplies from reaching the little colony for several weeks.

Lane, White and Harriot left early on the morning of July 31 in a pinnace to examine the land on the mainland. Several miles into the Albemarle Sound they sailed along the south coast and away from the Dasamonqueponke village on the northern side of the sound.

After sailing about ten miles they came upon a river. As they turned into the river, one of the crewmen saw something he identified as an alligator. It turned out to be a large fish commonly referred to as a carp, but the river retained the name of alligator from that day on.

As they sailed down the river, White made detailed sketches of everything he saw. After a few miles, three canoes approached with several Croatoans signaling to them with a friendly wave. They came alongside the pinnace and climbed aboard. They told Lane they had five small villages along the river. They said the game and fishing in the area was very good and fresh water was also available. It seemed that the Croatoans had spread out all over the peninsula.

Lane observed that there was fertile soil and lush vegetation in this area of the peninsula. They continued all the way down the river stopping at Croatoan villages and paying their respects as well as getting a lay of land. As they explored further, they noticed pine, cypress and juniper trees along the river's edge as well as in the interior. It crossed Lane's mind that the discovery of those trees could offer new colonists an industry exporting this wood since the material was excellent for manufacturing shingles. He made an entry of this finding in his journal.

Once Grenville and Amadas sailed out of the inlet and into the ocean, Amadas sailed north toward the Chesapeake Bay. Barlowe had informed him of his experiences when he had sailed up the bay the year before so he was prepared for what he might find.

Since the natives at the mouth of the bay appeared to be friendly according to Barlowe, Amadas decided that that would be his first stop. It was a three-day trip up the coast to the mouth of the bay. When the land on the eastern side of the bay appeared, Amadas sailed in that direction.

When they were a few hundred yards off the shoreline they continued to sail north. Eventually they came to the Chesapeake Indian town of Skicoak. Amadas had a crewman aboard, who had learned a little Algonquian on the 1585 expedition, to act as translator.

Amadas learned after speaking with the Chesapeake that they were governed by the Great War Chief Wahunsunacock (Powhatan) who lived up a great river on the other side of the bay. The river the Skicoak chief mentioned is today referred to as the York.

After visiting with the Skicoak's for a few days, they continued their sail up the bay and crossed over to the west side. Eventually, they came to another river that Barlowe had named after the tribe that he encountered about ten miles up on the north side.

Amadas knew they were running low on fresh water, so it was decided to pay the Rappahannocks a visit. About two miles from the village, they were greeted by ten or so canoes paddling toward him and they gave peaceful signs. They turned in the direction of the village, escorting the Ark Royal to their village. The village stretched along the shoreline for about a half-mile.

Amadas had a jolly boat lowered and Amadas, two soldiers and the crewman who spoke Algonquian rowed ashore. They were greeted by an excited group of natives and were welcomed by a young woman who identified herself as Hurit. Standing to her left was the chief of the tribe, Pajackok. They inquired for the health of Barlowe, whom they considered a friend. They told Amadas the story about how Barlowe returned Hurit from her kidnappers across the bay.

After spending two days with the Rappahannock, Amadas decided that he should leave the Chesapeake and rendezvous with Grenville in the Atlantic near the island of Sao Miguel.

Lane, White and Harriot sailed a pinnace back up the Alligator River and into the Albemarle Sound. They hugged the southern side to elude the northern villages. They passed the village of the Pomeiock and were invited to come ashore. Lane decided that he would accept their invitation, but he told the soldiers to have their weapons at the ready.

When they entered the village they were greeted by the chief and were offered some freshly cooked dog, which they accepted. They were told that the Croatoans had moved into their hunting grounds and were competing for the game. Lane sensed that a war was about to begin. He didn't acknowledge that they were on peaceful terms with the Croatoans, but if a war was to develop, he would take arms with them.

After trading several trinkets with the Pomeiock, Lane, White and Harriot boarded the 'pinnace' and continued their sail up the sound. When they reached the area where a river wound its way from the west and into the sound, they sailed up that river about a half mile where the village of the Weapemeoc Confederation was located.

They were invited ashore to feast with them. Through some talks with these friendly natives, they advised the English to abandon Roanoke Island and settle with them along the river. Lane told them that he would take their suggestion under consideration and discuss it with his chief. When he referred to his chief, he was referring to Raleigh.

They stayed with the Weapemeoc for a week while White sketched the area indicating the topography. Lane and Harriot took a jolly boat and rowed across the Sound to the other shore to visit with the Secota, who were friendly since the last English expedition provided them with much needed supplies.

The Secota had broken their alliance with Wingina and were ready to stand alone. They wanted the English to stand with them. At that point, Lane didn't want to involve the English in an Indian war, so he politely refused.

They bid goodbye to the Weapemeoc a few days later, and then sailed down the Albemarle Sound and into the Pamlico Sound. Once in that sound, they turned south and sailed up to the Pamlico River. They had heard from Wanchese on the return trip from England that there was a war like tribe on the shores of that river and they were led by a chief, whom they called Menatonon. He told the English that Menatonon might be relied upon to trade for food if they were approached in a peaceful manner.

Wanchese had devised a diabolical plan to send the colonists into the clutches of the powerful Chowanocs. When Lane entered the village, he immediately sensed danger. Before the warriors had a chance to surround him and his party, he identified the *weroance's* son, grabbed hold of the young warrior and with a knife to his throat backed slowly to the shoreline and into the jolly boat.

The young man's name was Skiko. When Lane and company arrived back at Roanoke Island, Skiko told Lane through his interpreter Harriot, that Wingina (who at the time had changed his name to Pemisapan, meaning "one who vigilantly watches"), had taken a middle course, removing his people from Dasamonqueponke to Dasemunkepeuc further up the Albemarle Sound, and cutting Lane off from any food supplies they had been trading.

After a few weeks, Lane not only met with Menatonon and survived, but the Chowanoc *weroance's* son Skiko, (a hostage) told the colonists of a land called Chaunis Temoantan, beyond Tuscarora territory where valuable copper was mined. Lane believed that it was imperative that he locate the copper mine and have White locate it on a map. This would be valuable information to carry back to England and share with Raleigh.

There was no time to lose. Supplies were running low and there were 107 men to feed. Lane put together a company of six soldiers, four crewmen, White, Harriot, and of course Skiko to lead the way. They took with them supplies for three weeks, since according Skiko they should be able to make the round trip during that time frame.

Lane asked Barlowe to take command in his absence. It was now late August and the weather was cooperating.

Lane and the expedition left early on the morning of August 25 and began their sail up the sound in the pinnace. Their destination was the Neuse-Pamlico peninsula in order to meet up with the Tuscarora to renew their supplies if necessary.

The day after Lane left to discover the copper mine that he was told by Skiko existed, Barlowe put one John Cotsmur in charge of the colony and the Mary Stark slowly slipped out of the little harbor on Roanoke Island. He had secret orders from Raleigh to explore the Chesapeake Bay and locate sassafras trees that might be growing there. He had instructed Barlowe to bring back to England a cargo of the leaves.

While Lane was searching for copper, Barlowe was on a sassafras hunt.

After sailing three days north along the American coast, they reached the mouth of the Chesapeake Bay and the river (later to be called James) flowing into it. Barlowe didn't sail this river the first time he explored the bay, but he was curious that it might contain the sassafras that he was searching.

Ten miles up the river and hugging the south side, he observed sassafras trees growing along the shoreline for miles. It was a mother load and more sassafras than he had ever seen.

Lane's expedition located the Neuse River and began to sail west. About seven miles up this impressive river was a Tuscarora village. He dropped anchor close to the shoreline. The water depth along this river was very deep and stretched almost to the land. The Tuscarora *weroance* Otetiani raised his arm in friendship. The Tuscaroras had heard that the English had been living with the Croatoans, off and on. They had further heard that a few of the English had taken Croatoan women as their wives. Otetiani and Lane communicated in sign language, since Harriot only spoke the Algonquian tongue and the Tuscarora's spoke Iroquoian.

Lane indicated that he had heard there was a copper mine nearby as he pointed to the copper rings in Otetiani's ear. He shook his head in the negative. Otetiani drew a crude map in the dirt that the copper came from a tribe a hundred or so miles into the mainland. He told Lane in his sign language that he had traded for the copper rings many moons ago. That the copper mine did not exist in his territory.

Lane understood now that Skiko had exaggerated the location of the mine and had caused him many days of unnecessary travel. It goes without saying that he was very unhappy with Skiko for taking him on this superfluous trip. The truth was that Skiko was hoping to escape while traveling and go back to his people. Lane put two and two together and figured out Skiko's reason for his deception. He placed two of the soldiers to guard him on the return trip. Lane decided to stop at the various villages on the way to Roanoke and pay his respects and trade for supplies.

Barlowe and his crew spent several days collecting the sassafras from the hundreds of trees that grew close to the shoreline of the James River. The final weight of the cargo was estimated at about two thousand pounds. He would have stayed and collected more, but they were discovered by a Powhatan war party and they rained down arrows upon them. One of the crew was struck in the neck by one of the arrows and died almost immediately. Barlowe was unable to retrieve the crewman's body as he and the crew ashore fired back upon the natives while the crew ferried back and forth in the jolly boat to the Mary Stark.

Once everyone else was safely aboard the ship, Barlowe had one of the cannons loaded and fired at the Powhatans who were firing arrows at the ship from the shoreline. The cannon ball had a direct hit on one of the natives, who appeared to be a *weroance,* taking his head clean off his shoulders. When the rest of the war party observed their leader killed by the cannon fire, they ran for the cover of the trees.

Barlowe had the anchor aweigh and unfurled the sails; he turned the ship toward the east and sailed down the river and into the bay.

Although he lost a crewmember, Barlowe considered the expedition a success. Since he was in the bay, Barlowe decided to sail back up to the Rappahannock and explore that river for the purpose of locating sassafras that he may have overlooked when they were there the last time. His destination was about fifty miles from his present location, and it took a full day and half sail to reach it.

When the Mary Stark arrived at the Rappahannock village, Barlowe and the crew were greeted by Pajackok, the chief of the tribe, and Hurit, the young woman they had met the year before when they had first sailed up the bay.

The crewman began to translate immediately and Barlowe offered presents to reestablish their friendship. Hurit was given a beautiful dress Barlowe had purchased for her when he was in London. It was a dress that was worn by all the fashionable women of London in 1580s. Pajackok was given a variety of tools and a hatchet made of the finest steel.

That night at the reunion feast, Barlowe had the crewman question Pajackok about any and all Indian settlements he might encounter if he continued up the bay. He learned that there was a great river to the north he called the Potomac, and that all the tribes along the south side of that river were under the Great War Chief, Powhatan, from the Paspahegh tribe to the south.

"All the tribes, including the Rappahannocks pay tribute to Powhatan, annually," Pajackok said through his translator.

Early the next morning, the Mary Stark slowly sailed back down the river and into the bay. Barlowe had the ship turn north and sailed about forty miles to the mouth of the big river the Rappahannock called Potomac.

As they sailed up this expansive river the Mary Stark encountered natives along the southern shoreline, waving to them with friendly gestures and requesting that they come ashore. Barlowe decided after his experience on the James River to exercise caution; therefore, he did not accept their invitations. He did observe, however, that he could identify sassafras trees close to the shoreline. He wrote of this discovery in his log.

When the Mary Stark reached the head waters of the river, Barlowe had the crew drop anchor. Along with four soldiers and four crewmen, Barlowe boarded a jolly boat and they all rowed to the north shore. There wasn't any sign of human activity, but in addition to observing signs of a wide variety of wild life in the area, it was flourishing with sassafras trees.

Shortly after they went ashore one of the soldiers shot a deer. After the animal was skinned and gutted, the meat was loaded into the jolly boat and taken back to the ship. The ship sent over another jolly boat with empty kegs to collect fresh water for the return trip.

After wandering about a half-mile into the woods and finding a fresh water spring, the party turned and returned to the beach. Barlowe mentioned to one of the crew that in his opinion the location would be a nice place to someday build a city. They all boarded the jolly boats, returned to the ship and began their trip down the river.

About five miles from where the river emptied into the bay, Barlowe decided to allow a few of the natives standing along the shoreline to board the Mary Stark. These friendly natives also spoke the Algonquian language and they indicated to Harriot that they were overwhelmed with what they saw aboard the ship.

Barlowe and his first mate John Harris gave their Indian guests the grand tour. There were three Indians in the visiting party and one was a woman. She was a chief that was referred to as a *weroansqua* ("woman chief").

Barlowe was struck by her natural beauty and for a brief moment he wrestled with the idea of taking her back to England with him. He discussed this possibility with Harris and after a short discussion; they both agreed that it wouldn't be a good idea to kidnap her. They gave the visiting Indians presents in order to establish future friendly relations if and when they returned in the future.

Barlowe had the sails unfurled and the anchor aweigh and they continued down the Potomac and into the bay. They turned south and headed back to Roanoke.

He could hardly wait to return to England and present to Raleigh his valuable cargo. He sailed down the coast making his destination Roanoke Island.

It was a three-day sail down the Chesapeake Bay before he reached the Outer Banks and the inlet that would allow him to enter the Pamlico Sound. They sailed another hour and the island of Roanoke came into view. As he drifted slowly into the little harbor, he was greeted by several of the colonists standing on the shoreline anticipating his arrival.

The men on the island informed Barlowe that Lane had not returned from his search for the copper mine that Skiko had described to him.

One of the men, John Cotsmur, whom Barlowe left in charge, told him that some of the Dasemunkepeuc natives had been raiding the Roanoke colony at night and one was recently caught in the act. After they interrogated the captive, he informed them that Pemisapan (who was previously named Wingina) was collecting warriors from the villages up the Albemarle Sound to attack the colony and kill all its occupants.

Barlowe took this information under advisement. After discussing it with one of his officers and Cotsmur, they decided to act before being attacked. After further interrogation of the captured native, it was learned that Pemisapan was living in the village of the Cotan twenty-five miles up the Albemarle Sound. Barlowe also decided that Skiko had told Lane a lie about the existence of the copper mine, so it would give Pemisapan time to collect the number of warriors he needed to overwhelm the colonists.

What Barlowe didn't know was that when Lane visited a Croatoan village, he was told that several of their Croatoans brothers were going on a trading mission to the Cotan village. The Croatoans knew that the English were suspicious of Pemisapan, and they further knew that the English at some point may attack them.

The Croatoan chief had requested the English to give the Croatoan traders something that would identify them in the event the English were to attack one of Pemisapan's villages while they were there trading. Lane gave the Croatoans a patch with a cross in the center to wear.

"When the English see that patch they will know that you are our Croatoan friends," Lane told the chief.

Unfortunately, Barlowe was not aware of this friendly sign the Croatoans would be displaying. He gathered twenty-five soldiers armed with Harquebus's and swords and they sailed for the Cotan village.

It was early evening when the Mary Stark sailed up the Albemarle Sound. Barlowe decided to anchor about a mile down the sound and to attack the Cotan village at night.

Using all the stealth they could employ, the anchor was lowered and the soldiers were ferried by jolly boats to the shoreline. The soldiers moved quietly through the woods until they came to an opening and a Cotan corn field lay before them.

The soldiers spread out as they reached the perimeter of the village. All was quiet and the Cotan warrior who was on guard duty was sitting up against a tree, asleep. One of the soldiers moved in behind him, cut his throat, and signaled to his comrades to come into the village proper.

When one of the soldiers entered a longhouse a woman screamed. All hell broke out as native men and women ran in all directions. What Barlowe didn't know was that among the Cotan were Croatoans who had come to trade as they had mentioned to Lane a few days before. Some of the Croatoans kept pointing to the patch with the cross they were wearing, but it was dark and unrecognizable. By the time Barlowe's men finally realized that some of the natives were Croatoan many had already been wounded and killed.

Pemisapan ran out of one of the houses and attempted to stab a soldier. The soldier stood aside and shot Pemisapan in the leg. Pemisapan ran into the woods and hid in the darkness. Barlowe had all the women and children rounded up and put into a big circle at the center of the village under the guard of five soldiers. The soldiers herded the Cotan warriors that had surrendered and the ones who were wounded into a longhouse and kept them there under guard as well.

Early the next morning and just as the sun was coming up, an Irish soldier by the name of Edward Nugent went into the woods in search of Pemisapan. Along the edge of the woods where Pemisapan had run the night before was a trail of blood. He found Pemisapan sitting against a tree falling in and out of consciousness from loss of blood. Twenty minutes later, Nugent came out of the woods holding the severed head of Pemisapan.

A day after Barlowe had returned to Roanoke Island, an ambassador representing all the tribes along the sound came to the island and brought tribute. The ambassador informed Barlowe through his translator that his people didn't want war with the English and they would help them in any way they could.

Barlowe didn't believe this subservient native, but he didn't want war. He accepted the tribute that was offered and sent the ambassador on his way.

Barlowe was now anxious to return to England with his cargo, so he put Mr. Cotsmur in charge of the colony until Lane returned. He told the colonists that he would be amenable to take back to England five of the colonists who wished to go. Ten men raised their hands. He had them draw lots and five were selected. Everyone boarded the Mary Stark and she sailed out into the Atlantic.

A few days later, Lane returned to a very unhappy and hungry colony. He was beside himself as to what he should do. He was told about Barlowe's attacking the Cotan and killing their *weroance*, Pemisapan. Lane did not receive this information gladly. He believed that if he had previously any chance trading with the natives up the Albemarle Sound, now it was not going to be an alternative.

Just as Lane was feeling at an all time low and wondering what he was going to do, a fleet of twenty-three ships led by Francis Drake, and including the future Virginia governor, Sir Thomas Gates, arrived unexpectedly. Drake gave Lane one of his supply ships.

Now, Lane believed that all of his problems had been solved.

Within a few hours after Drake's arrival a large storm (probably a hurricane) ravaged the island and the ship with the supplies, Drake had so generously gave to Lane, washed out to sea and was lost.

After two days, the storm had ended and Lane made a decision to abandon the island and take advantage of Drake's offer to evacuate him and the colonists.

Before the ship was to leave, however, Lane believed that Skiko needed to be punished for sending him on the wild goose chase in search of a non-existent copper mine. He held a short trial and Skiko was found guilty of deception, and wasting valuable time and money. He was condemned to death by hanging.

Two soldiers tied his hands behind his back and had him stand on a chair. Lane had the rope thrown over a tree and put a noose around his neck. One of the soldiers kicked away the chair. It took Skiko about twenty minutes to die by strangulation. They left the body hanging for the other natives to see as a warning not to deceive the English.

Lane and the colonists collected their belongings and boarded several of Drake's ships. Drake had the ships aweigh anchor and they sailed back to England.

A few weeks after Drake and Lane set sail for England, a relief mission arrived under the command of Grenville. He had captured two Spanish ships and relieved them of their supplies. When they sailed into the little bay at Roanoke Island, they found the palisades doors wide open and the area abandoned. Still hanging from a tree was the body of Skiko. Grenville wasn't aware for the reason of this execution, but he surmised that Skiko had betrayed Lane in some way and was discovered.

After some discussion among Grenville and his officers, it was decided to remove the body and give it a Christian burial. After much consternation and staying on the island for another week, Grenville decided to set sail for England. It was decided to leave fifteen soldiers on the island to guard the existing facilities. They unloaded enough provisions to last the soldiers for a year.

Since Lane's leaving with Drake and Grenville deciding to leave as well, this overall disaster ended the first attempt to establish an English colony in America.

CHAPTER VI

Amadas was the first of the colony ships to sail into Plymouth harbor. It was followed by a Spanish merchant ship that he had captured while privateering with Grenville in the Atlantic. The ship and its cargo were valued at one hundred and fifty thousand pounds.

Raleigh was given a half day notice that Amadas was going to be arriving from a fast military vessel that had been sailing off the coast. He estimated Amadas time of arrival and made his way down to the dock as the Ark Royal drifted into the harbor.

Through his spyglass, Amadas spotted Raleigh standing on the pier and he assumed that he was waiting for him. No sooner had the anchor been dropped, Amadas had a jolly boat lowered and had two of his crew row him to meet Raleigh on the pier.

Raleigh extended his hand to greet him as Amadas climbed up the latter that was attached to the pier. The first thing out of Raleigh's mouth was "So tell me Captain, what's the news about my colony in America?"

Raleigh rested his arm over Amadas shoulder and they slowly walked toward the inn. Amadas began by telling Raleigh about the terrible storm they'd encountered off the coast of Africa.

"We were separated for two weeks and I rightly decided to make my way to Puerto Rico and the Port of Mosquetal, where we had all agreed to meet in the event that a storm was encountered. Captain Grenville was already there when I arrived. Captain Grenville was making repairs on his ship," he said.

"Did all the ships finally arrive?" Raleigh inquired.

"After three weeks all the ships from our original fleet sailed into the Puerto Rico port, except the supply ship, Primrose. We assumed that she probably sunk in the storm. So on the fourth week, we all sailed for America and to the island of Roanoke," Amadas informed him.

"What landfall did you encounter upon arriving in America?" Raleigh asked.

"We stopped first at a barrier island the natives called Wococon, that according to Fernandez was about eighty miles from the island of Roanoke," Amadas responded.

Amadas went on to tell Raleigh that when they came to an inlet near the barrier island, Fernandez was confident from his previous experience entering inlets along that coast. "He decided taking soundings wasn't necessary when it was high tide," Amadas said, "So, when the Tiger was about halfway through the inlet she ran aground. As a result of that grounding all the supplies on the ship were spoiled. After we did an inventory of what supplies we had on the other ships, it was determined we only had enough sustenance to feed the colonists for twenty days. After that time we were going to have to depend on trading with the local natives. Although that was probable, it wasn't likely. We had been told by the Croatoans that the area was experiencing a long drought. This also made the trading with the natives for food dubious at best."

Amadas took a long pause before he said, "I don't want to criticize your cousin, Sir Richard Grenville, but sometimes it became difficult to follow his lead. There were some decisions he made, in my opinion, that were not in the best interest with establishing a safe colony."

"Can you give me an example of when Richard made a bad decision that would have affected the safety of the colony?" Raleigh asked in a somewhat defensive tone.

"When we arrived and landed on the island of Wococon and later ran aground, the Tiger was in need of repair. Captain Grenville decided that this would be a good time to explore the Pamilico River and pay his respects to the tribes whose villages were located along the shoreline up that body of water. He toured the Secotan Villages of Pomiock, Aquascogoc, and Secota while identifying other villages around the shores of Pamlico."

Amadas took a slight pause before continuing. "Captain Grenville's soldiers presented an impressive military force to the Secotan tribes and intimidated them into trading for food. While we were touring, John White went to work and made various sketches of the individual natives, their villages, the topography of the land and river. The captain knew that our supplies were very limited and he imposed on the *weroance* of the various tribes for assistance. However, as I mentioned previously, there had been a prolonged drought in the area and food was at a minimum. Later this food shortage caused a conflict between the Secotans and us."

Amadas took another slight pause before he said, "Another problem developed after we left the villages: small pox broke out among all the natives. They reasoned and rightfully so, that we were transmitting that disease to them. But the one thing that implicated me personally was when we finally reached Roanoke Island, one of the soldiers was missing a tin cup from the last village we had visited. Captain Grenville ordered me to return to that village and retrieve the cup. His orders were if the cup is not returned then burn the village to the ground. When I arrived at that village, all of the natives denied knowing anything about the cup. So, I followed his orders, reluctantly, and I burned the village down. Obeying that order didn't endear us to the local tribes in the area," Amadas said as he took another big swallow of his ale.

"You're absolutely right. We should restrain ourselves from doing anything in America that doesn't establish good relations with the natives. I will address this problem with Captain Grenville as soon as he returns," Raleigh stated as he too took a long swallow of the ale as well.

Raleigh could now see that putting his cousin in charge of the expedition was a fatal mistake. Everything that Amadas told him added to his belief that the expedition was a failure. This was going to infuriate the Queen when she learned how much money was lost because of the incompetence on Grenville's part and for his (Raleigh's) recommending him to lead.

If Grenville was there at that moment, Raleigh thought, *I could put my hands around his throat and strangle him.*

The only thing Raleigh could do at this point was to wait for the rest of the expedition to return. *At least Amadas had captured a Spanish supply ship and that would help in defraying some of the expenses. If Barlowe returns with another cargo of sassafras that would also help,* he thought.

He sat and talked with Amadas for the rest of the afternoon and the two of them got quite intoxicated.

Five weeks later, word reached Raleigh that Lane arrived on Francis Drake's ship and was in port at Plymouth. He sent word to Lane to come to London immediately for a meeting. The fact that Lane had abandoned the colony made Raleigh furious.

Lane knew he was in trouble from the language contained in the letter he received from Raleigh. Lane believed, however, that he had good reasons to present for his abandonment of his post.

In addition to that, there was word of a copper mine to the west of Virginia. It may take a planned expedition to reach it, but he was sure it was there. Most of the natives that he came into contact with were wearing copper ornaments. He had traded for some of these copper items especially for the purpose of showing them to Raleigh.

Lane also knew that Manteo was in London. He intended to take him to the meeting with Raleigh. Manteo may be able to provide more details on the location of the copper mine.

Drake decided to go along with Lane to London. Drake wanted to report his findings about the Spanish in the Caribbean. There was news circulating from a Spanish pilot named Pedro Diaz who had been captured by Grenville and escaped to St. Augustine. After being interrogated in St. Augustine by its governor, he was sent to Havana.

Diaz told the Havana Governor that the English were planning a colony on Roanoke Island for the purpose of giving safe harbor to privateering ships. Diaz reported that the land was wretchedly poor on the island but that the soil on the mainland, which he could only see from a distance, appeared fertile and well wooded.

He further reported that when they arrived, they found an Indian hanging from a tree in an otherwise empty colony. Diaz said, "Grenville remained for several days and left fifteen men, four pieces of artillery and supplies for one year."

When Lane and Drake reached London, Drake went directly to Buckingham Palace to meet with the Queen. Lane stopped off briefly at his residence to inform his family that he had arrived home. After refreshing himself and having a good meal, he reluctantly made his way to Raleigh's home on the Thames.

Raleigh's servant answered the door and showed Lane into the study where he was to wait. Shortly, Raleigh appeared and sat down across from him and began asking him why he had abandoned the colony. Lane went through a long list of reasons, beginning with the grounding of the Tiger. He said that Grenville had alienated the Indians to the point of declaring war.

Lane said that Barlowe raided the major Indian village on the Albemarle Sound when he learned that Roanoke Island was going to be attacked. He killed the chief and dozens of others including many Croatoans, who were friends with the English.

"When Drake arrived with supplies, he graciously gave us a ship loaded with everything we would need only later to have it washed out to sea in a storm. The men were restless and disappointed. They had been told before leaving on the expedition that they would find gold, silver, and pearls. None of that came to fruition. There was nowhere else to go but to return home with Drake. To have remained there under those conditions would have resulted in a death sentence." As Lane finished his explanation, he bowed his head and stared at the floor.

Raleigh offered Lane a glass of sherry. He accepted. As Raleigh was pouring the drinks, a knock came at the door. Raleigh's servant showed Manteo into the study.

When Raleigh turned and saw Manteo, he poured a third glass for his Indian friend. Manteo sat next to Lane and told pretty much the same story as he knew it.

Manteo explained to Raleigh how Wanchese disappeared from the settlement shortly after they arrived. He didn't lose any time rushing to have a conference with Wingina. He told Wingina that Grenville was not to be trusted. Manteo explained how Grenville had spent time visiting with Wingina's enemies the Piemacum, Aquascogoc and the Secotan. Wingina became infuriated and declared war on the English.

The three of them sat quietly and drank their sherry. Raleigh wondered aloud when Grenville would arrive. Amadas had told him that he believed that Grenville was going back to Roanoke and drop off the supplies he had privatized from the Spanish, but he wasn't sure. They had gotten separated in an Atlantic storm.

When Drake arrived at the palace, the Queen was overjoyed to see him. Everyone believed that she was infatuated with him, but it has never been learned if they had a physical relationship. Of course, Raleigh was another story that we will get into later.

Drake sat for hours entertaining the Queen with his many stories. She invited him to dine with her and he didn't leave until late in the evening. She told Drake at dinner that Raleigh was going to brief her on the colony situation the next day. She was expecting unpleasant news. Drake told her the little he knew which wasn't very much.

When Raleigh arrived at the palace around noon the next day, the Queen had left orders that he was to be immediately directed to her private quarters. When he entered the room, all of the Queen's 'ladies in waiting' were excused to allow the Queen and Raleigh privacy.

They spent an hour and half behind closed doors and when they finally merged, the Queen was giggling like a school girl and leaning on Raleigh's shoulder. She ordered a private lunch to be served in her room.

After another half an hour of flirting and making small talk, the Queen finally got down to business. The Queen took Raleigh by the hand and walked him out onto a small balcony adjacent to the room. Looking out over the landscape she asked a pointed question, "Why did we lose so much money on the expedition to America?

You had assured me that there were gold and silver deposits there that could be loaded on the ships and brought back to England."

"I've learned of several reasons for the failure of the expedition Your Majesty. First, Ralph Lane's desertion of his post and Sir Richard Grenville's failure to resupply him were probably the biggest contributions to the overall loss of finances and failure of establishing a colony. Grenville's privateering had produced far less returns on our investment and produced considerably less than it did on his last mission," he candidly said.

"I don't need to remind you that the venture's losses and the public gossip will make it difficult to finance another expedition. You will need a less expensive way to maintain your charter, which as you know will expire in four years to establish a permanent colony," she said in a matter of fact business tone.

"Your Majesty, I've given this situation a lot of thought and I believe I have designed a plan that will accomplish everything we had previously discussed about how to establish and maintain a successful colony in America. Instead of having a colony staffed with soldiers and gentlemen adventurers, whose interest in gold, silver, and a quick return home are their only interest, I'm going to suggest that the colonists be planters families. I will select people such as artisans and subsistence farmers and put them on their own land. These farmers would be sent out to harvest sassafras which would be financially advantageous to everyone. I intend to replace all of the past leaders of the past two expeditions with one reliable individual," he said with a tone of confidence.

"And who might this reliable individual be, Sir Walter?" she inquired.

"The person I have in mind Your Majesty is John White, who has been to America twice before and has studied the land and the rivers along the coast," he said.

"But Mr. White is an artist and not an expedition leader or sea captain," she said with a certain amount of doubt.

"That's correct Your Majesty, but he knows the land and from what I've been told by Captain's Barlowe and Amadas; he is a natural leader.

"This plan must be kept in complete confidence and only revealed to the few active members of the expedition. I'm going to spread a rumor that England is planning a military expedition on the Chesapeake Bay. The rumor will be spread throughout the Court that the expedition under Mr. White will be the establishment of the city of Raleigh."

"After the expedition under Mr. White sails to America, we will let it leak to the Spanish that Sir Richard Grenville is sailing to the Chesapeake to supply Mr. White. The Spanish will concentrate on that area until we can relocate our farmers to an out-of-the-way and secret location on the mainland. Once they are settled, they can begin farming the sassafras which will fill our coffers with revenue as well as offset some of the expenses we have incurred so far with the other expeditions," he proudly said.

"Sir Walter, you're a genius. I guess that is why I'm so in love with you," she said with a twinkle in her eye.

She took Raleigh by the hand and they returned to spend the rest of the afternoon in the privacy of her room.

Several days later, John White was summoned to Raleigh's residence. After some ambiguous and mundane conversation, Raleigh got down to business.

"Mr. White, the Queen and I have decided to finance another expedition to America and we have selected you to lead that endeavor," he said in a matter-of-fact business like delivery.

White looked completely shocked. "But Sir, I appreciate your confidence in me, and please excuse my saying so, but, I don't have any leadership experience to take over such an important and expensive undertaking," he said demonstrating the meekness in his personality.

Raleigh explained that the expedition to America this time was going to be somewhat different from the one he experienced the last time he was there.

"The colonists that you'll be taking with you will not be soldiers and gentlemen of fortune, but artisans and farmers. You will not be looking for gold and silver to return to England, but will be farming sassafras. After the colonists are told of the real reason for being in America, each colonist will be told that they will be given five hundred acres of land to own and farm. In return, I will ask each colonist to pay for their transportation to America and to purchase supplies for one year. You will not share the true purpose of this expedition until you reach America. We will also spread the rumor that your first stop in America will be Roanoke Island for the purpose of picking up the fifteen soldiers Grenville had left there before he sailed. I will give you sealed orders before you sail to be opened and executed when you arrive on Roanoke Island." When Raleigh finished, he just stared at White to anticipate any questions he might have.

White took a long pause before he finally said, "I think I completely understand the mission, Sir, and I will carry out my duties just as you so clearly described and outlined."

"Good day, Mr. White, and report back to me once a week on your progress. I'll look forward to those meetings," he said with a smile and a handshake.

The next day, White began recruiting future colonists immediately.

Raleigh gave White broad authority over the nine of his associates to govern Virginia; however, Raleigh would continue to exercise overall authority. To help White recruit men who would help him lead, Raleigh provided coats of arms for the governor and his associates.

White recruited associates and artisans from the City of London guilds, such as his own Painter Strainers Guild and the Tilers Guild of his son-in-law, Ananias Dare. Three associates were to remain behind to represent the colony's commercial interests and lobby for additional financial support.

With Raleigh's support and enticements, White was able to recruit 117 men and women who were willing to live in Virginia. London at that time was not a very pleasant or healthy place to live, and future colonists concluded that living in America had to be an improvement to their health and way of life.

All in all, there were eleven married couples without children and two couples with one child each. The rest were eighty single men and seven single women, two sons or younger brothers and three other boys.

The overall group was made up of yeoman, husbandmen, gentlemen, a sheriff, a lawyer, a vestryman, a goldsmith, a tailor, scholars and prison inmates. Two of these potential colonists had been to Roanoke on the last expeditions. The single women were related to other potential colonists by marriage and many of the other potential colonists were related in some fashion. It was advertised by White that other colonists would join them after the colony was established and provide wives for the single men.

Most of these Roanoke colonists hailed from London and or the west side of England of Devon and Cornwall. Many of the potential colonists had been at one time or another was tenant farmers before resettling in London. It was the wool manufacturing that had produced jobs in the city; the enclosed sheep pastures had reduced cropland and the need for tenant farmers. With the five hundred acres provided to each individual, it was not unreasonable for the colonists to become tobacco plantation owners as well as harvesting the valuable sassafras.

One of the drawbacks of the recruiting process was the Puritans that were added to the list of passengers. This was going to cause some consternation, once they began expressing their religious beliefs and practices when they reached Roanoke.

After months of planning and preparation, the potential colonists assembled in Portsmouth, England and began boarding ships. They sailed on April 26, 1587. The ships were the Lion of 120 tons piloted by Simon Fernandez, an unnamed flyboat under Captain Spicer, a pinnace under Captain Stafford, and three additional pinnaces under unnamed captains.

After sailing for eight days they stopped over on the Isle of Wright where White and Fernandez coordinated plans with Sir George Carey to have his fleet bring additional settlers to Virginia while on a privateering venture to the West Indies.

It had been planned to bring Carey's fleet eventually to meet up with Grenville's in the Chesapeake Bay. They expected that the Spanish would be searching for a naval installation and or the city of Raleigh that had been leaked to the Spanish. The plan was after Carey dropped off the other settlers at Roanoke; he would proceed to the Chesapeake and assist Grenville with capturing the Spanish ships they expected to show up there.

For whatever reason, White's ships returned to Portsmouth on May 5 to relay to Raleigh some information he obtained while on the Isle of Wright. After meeting with Raleigh, the expedition left port on the May 8 and departed for the West Indies.

At that time, Francis Drake was busy raiding Spanish ships at Cadiz that had the effect of delaying the dreaded arrival of the Spanish Armada.

The colonists were anxious to reach Virginia in time for the spring planting, but the captains and crews of the ships had another objective. They were intent on privateering for a while. White continually complained to Fernandez about the delays, and he often complained in his narrative about Fernandez's antagonism toward him and neglect of the colony's mission.

White expressed his anger to anyone who would listen. When Fernandez abandoned their distressed flyboat near Portugal and failed to acquire livestock, fruit, salt and adequate fresh water in the West Indies, it distressed him even further.

Darbie Glaven, an acquaintance of Fernandez whom he had confided in, informed the Spanish everything he knew about the colony's plans when they stopped in Puerto Rico to replenish their water supply.

After a few more delays, on July 22 two of the three ships finally arrived at the inlet nearest Roanoke Island.

Fernandez was instructed by Raleigh before he sailed to spread the story that the purpose for landing on Roanoke Island was only to relieve the men that had been left there by Grenville.

When they finally arrived on Roanoke Island, the men that Grenville left behind had disappeared, with the exception of one house that displayed some fire damage there was there was no other evidence of violence. Their ship was anchored in the little bay and the colonists were ferried over to the little settlement and told to select housing. They were told that they would be remaining there for a short period of time.

Fernandez wrote in his log that his crew became belligerent and wanted to continue up the Chesapeake Bay without the settlers. The settlers were on the island and they refused to allow them back on the Lion. Of course, this was a fabrication that was invented by Raleigh to cover the real reason for this expedition.

When White returned to England several months later, he told a similar story that the settlers were left stranded on the island. That was also White's excuse for finally agreeing to return to England for additional supplies for the colony.

White reported that when they arrived at Roanoke, the palisades were down but many of the houses remained standing. He said that the surviving houses were soon repaired and several new cottages were built.

On July 25, Captain Edward Spicer's flyboat found its way to Roanoke Island. He brought along with him the rest of White's settlers and supplies.

Spicer had surprised Fernandez with his navigational skill in locating Roanoke, since he had never been there before. White said that Spicer's arrival displeased Fernandez who had expected that Spicer had either been captured, returned to England or had gone directly to the Chesapeake Bay.

On July 28, George Howe, one of the six associates who came on the expedition, was ambushed and killed while crabbing without armor or weapons. He was stuck with sixteen arrows and then clubbed to death with wooden swords. White suspected that the Secotan had come over from the Dasamonquepeuc mainland to hunt deer or to spy on the colony, and fled back to the mainland after killing Howe.

White became extremely concerned, so he sent Stafford, Manteo and twenty soldiers to the Croatoan mainland to learn what had happened to Howe and Grenville's men. The other part of the mission was to renew their previous friendship with the Croatoan.

Because Barlowe and his men killed by mistake some of the Croatoan when raiding Wingina's village, the Croatoans were frightened by the arrival of armed Englishmen and ran from them.

After Manteo settled the frightened Croatoans by calling them out in their own language, they pleaded with Stafford not to take the little corn they had left. The year before, Stafford had led a group of Lane's men to Croatan Island in 1586 when food was scarce on Roanoke Island. He informed them through Manteo that he appreciated their plight and would not take their corn. He told them the purpose for being there was to renew the friendship they had enjoyed with the Croatan in the past.

After stating a few more consolations, Stafford asked if they knew who had killed George Howe. They told him that Howe was killed by a remnant of Wingina's warriors. There were also warriors from the upper tribes such as the Secotan from Aquascogoc, Pomeiock and the Secota villages. They further told Stafford that these same Indians had launched a thirty warrior attack on the men left behind by Grenville. Knowing that they could not defeat the Englishmen when they were armed and alert, the Secotan resorted to trickery such as Barlowe had used against them.

Two Secotan warriors who appeared to be unarmed called out as friends and two English captains came out to greet them. They held and clubbed one of the Englishman to death as the second Englishman escaped into the fort to alert the others. When the Secotan set fire to one of the houses the Englishmen had taken cover in, the men seized any weapons they could find and ran out to engage the Secotan. Hiding behind trees, the Secotan fired a hail of arrows at the Englishmen. A second Englishman died of an arrow through his mouth and the others suffered injuries. The survivors retreated to the creek where they had left their boat. They picked up the four soldiers who had been away digging for oysters and rowed to Bodie Island. This was a little island just off Roanoke Island. The Croatoan said they remained there for a few days, but they eventually left. The Croatoan lost track of them after that.

At White's instructions, Stafford told the Croatoans that John White wanted to make peace with the Secotan. White asked the Croatoans to invite the *weroance's* from the villages of Secota, Aquascogoc and Pomeiock to a meeting with him. The Croatoans replied that they would try to bring the Secotan to a conference at Roanoke Island within seven days or bring their answer.

A few weeks passed and the Secotan never appeared.

Apparently, Wanchese had taken over the confederation of the Secotan and he feared that his small group of warriors would be attacked. He further decided to move farther west and out of the reach of these English invaders. The Secotan had left behind fields of ripe corn, tobacco, and melons. When the Croatoans learned that Secotan had abandoned their villages, they hurried to the different locations along the Albemarle Sound and claimed the areas for themselves. Afterward, they brought much of the produce that they inherited to the English to trade.

After, the Secotan abandoned the land the Croatoans now controlled, not only the land now known as the Dare Mainland, but the land north of the Albemarle Sound as well. Manteo was the new authority of the Croatoan and he had the ability to control it with the assistance of an alliance of well-armed Englishmen. Manteo also introduced the Church of England to the Croatoan people.

It had been decided that before Fernandez would explore the Chesapeake Bay and then sail back to England, he would accompany

White and company to explore possible locations to resettle the colonists. In addition, White wanted to get Ananias Dare educated to the overall plan that had been devised by Raleigh in his sealed instructions to him before sailing. These instructions outlined the main purpose of the colony was to farm sassafras.

Therefore, White, Fernandez, Manteo, and Ananias boarded a pinnace and sailed up the Albemarle Sound and down the Alligator River. Manteo had been asked by White to go along as their interpreter. They spent over a week locating sites where the sassafras trees were abundant.

Eventually, they located the five locations where the Croatoans had established little villages along the river of about thirty to fifty individuals. The land was already cleared. It was decided to divide the colonists into groups of about twenty or less and locate them with the Croatoans to begin farming activities. At these locations, in the opinion of White and Ananias agreed that the soil was of excellent composition and the sassafras was abundant. There was one location just below the mouth of the river, where they all agreed to build a small fort to defend against anyone attempting to invade their little community. The fort would be manned by the soldiers who were among the colonists.

They met many of the Croatoans who had moved onto this land the year before. They told White that there was excellent hunting of deer and rabbit; however, they were competing with the Tuscarora for the hunting rights. Apparently, the drought had caused many of the animals to leave the Neuse River area and they were in desperate need of meat. The Croatoans said that when they would meet the Tuscarora while hunting, sometimes those meetings would become violent. White discarded this as a minor problem. He knew that the Tuscarora could not defend themselves against his English fire power.

When they returned to Roanoke Island, White was confronted with another problem that was entirely different from finding locations for the colonists. It seems that the colonists whose religion was the Church of England decided to use one of the existing buildings for a church. This religion was in its infancy and it hadn't been that long since Henry the VIII had separated it from the Roman Catholic Church. As a result of this short period of time, the English Church continued many of the same practices and traditions of the Roman religion.

There were two Puritan families that had come to America with these colonists and were fanatical in their beliefs. They insisted on having a church that was plain in nature and without the Church of England's ceremonies. The two religions had come to an impasse and could not resolve their disagreements.

White knew that the Croatoans still had some of their tribe living on Croatan Island (Cape Hatteras). After attempting to mediate between the two groups, he reached the conclusion that there would be no compromise reached and the only thing left to do was to relocate the Puritans. He had them pack their things and prepare to leave.

Early the next morning they were put on a 'pinnace' with Manteo and taken to Croatan Island.

When they arrived, Manteo introduced them to the *weroance* and showed them the English housing that had been left behind by the English from the first and second trips.

Manteo returned to Roanoke Island and reported to White that it appeared to him that Puritans would fit in nicely living by themselves and practicing their religion in peace.

Fernandez was anxious to leave Roanoke Island to sail the

Chesapeake, ambush the Spanish ships, and then return to England with his trophies. White had a need for someone from the colony to return to England and return with the additional colonists and supplies, but no one would come forth and volunteer.

About the time White was attempting to recruit a colonist to accompany Fernandez, his daughter Elinor went into labor with her child. Elinor Dare was one of two women who were pregnant and had made the trip to America. Elinor had been five months into her pregnancy when they sailed.

On the August 18, Elinor Dare was gardening around the cabin that she and her husband Ananias shared when her water broke. She was ordered to bed by the mid wife. White was told that Elinor was in labor and giving birth to his grandchild.

White and Ananias waited the nearly twenty-four hours for Elinor to deliver the child. Elinor and Ananias named the little girl, "Virginia," after the name of the colony and in respect to her Majesty, Elizabeth.

White was relieved that this daughter and grandchild were alive and healthy. He spent a few days with Elinor and Virginia, but spent the majority of that time recruiting a volunteer to go with Fernandez.

Finally, and in desperation at the last minute, White decided to go himself.

He appointed Ananias Dare in charge of the colony in his absence.

White called Ananias to a meeting. "I will be back in six or seven months. In the meantime, I would like you to begin moving the colony to the Alligator River as we had previously discussed. I will leave you three 'pinnaces' to use to transport material to the Alligator River. This is going to be an arduous undertaking, but it's essential that it be done. I would also like you to begin the move as soon as I leave for England. When I return, if you have completed the move and are settled on the Alligator River, leave me a message confirming your location. Since the colonists will be living alongside the Croatoans, carve the word 'Croatan' on the palisade and I'll know where to find you. We don't want to give any other clues as to where the colony might be in the event the Spanish come by after you have moved. Please take care of my daughter and grandchild in my absence."

"You know you can depend on me, sir, to follow your orders to the letter," Ananias said with a certain amount of humility.

At the time, White wasn't aware that he would never see his daughter and granddaughter again.

On August 21, when Fernandez's sailors were finally finished unloading the three ships of supplies for the colony, they set sail.

CHAPTER VII

Ananias Dare had his orders. He knew exactly what he was supposed to do to relocate the colony. He was also aware of their mission: to establish a settlement along the Alligator River growing sassafras and other food to feed the colonists.

Fernandez gave his crew a respite while sailing in the Chesapeake and had his three ships anchored in a large cove just off the bay. He had allowed his crew to fish from one of their jolly boats. One of the sailors who were fishing noticed the sails of a large ship in the distance heading their way. They rowed back to the cove and informed Fernandez that they believed they saw a Spanish ship about a mile or two in the distance.

Fernandez went into action. He positioned his ship, the Lion, which was well-equipped with a cannon to line up at the mouth of the cove so that its portside was facing the bay. He waited until the Spanish ship passed the cove; the Lion opened fire while the flyboat raced toward the damaged vessel and boarded her.

There wasn't a lot of resistance from the Spanish and they surrendered almost immediately after being boarded. The Spanish ship was seriously damaged and was beginning to sink. The Spanish crew were loaded into life boats and set adrift. The English coveted as much plunder as they could carry and taking along the Spanish officers, they retreated to the safety of the Lion.

The Spanish officers were treated with respect and dignity according to their rank and were given accommodations aboard the English ships. The Spanish crew had rowed to the shoreline and stood looking on as the English ships sailed away. Fernandez knew that those crew members would probably not last a fortnight in that area of the bay, since it was infested with hostile natives.

After questioning the Spanish officers, Fernandez and White learned that Raleigh's plan to have the Spanish looking for the English colonists in the Chesapeake, and not in Virginia, was working as planned.

Shortly after this incident, the Lion and the other ships left the Chesapeake and set sail for England.

Two and a half months later and surviving a Mid Atlantic storm, they arrived at Plymouth Harbor.

As soon as they dropped their anchors, all three ships were boarded by Admiralty Officers. They were told that their ships were being impressed into the British Navy. England was now at war with Spain. The Spanish officers aboard the Lion were taken into custody for interrogation and were to be incarcerated for the duration of the war.

White immediately took transportation to London. It was imperative that he meet with Raleigh as soon as possible. There was so much activity in and around Plymouth; it was very difficult to get transportation to London due to the war. Men, sixteen years of age and older were being drafted into the army and navy. There was much consternation and it was rumored that England was going to be invaded by the Spanish. The English knew that if the Spanish were to take control of the country, the old church would be reinstituted and the inquisition would be inflicted upon them.

Eventually, and after much bribing, White was able to get transportation to London to see Raleigh. It took two days of travel and skirting blocked roads to finally reach his destination. Without losing a minute, he went right to Raleigh's residence. Once there, he was told that Raleigh was at the palace meeting with the Queen.

The palace was located about a half hour away. Once again, he had difficulty obtaining transportation. When he finally arrived at the Palace an hour and a half later, the guards at the gates were reluctant to admit him. But, after producing a document signed by Sir Walter Raleigh, he was escorted to a room where a meeting between Sir Francis Drake, Sir Walter Raleigh and the Queen was taking place.

When the three of them looked up from the table and saw White, they requested that he come in and take a seat.

The Queen began the questioning. "What are you doing here, Mr. White? I was told you were heading the organization of the colony in America."

"Yes Your Majesty and forgive me for interrupting your meeting with these honorable gentlemen, but this is a dire emergency. I was forced to leave my duties on the Roanoke Island to come here and beg for supplies and to transport back along with the additional colonists that we were promised," he stated in a voice laced with urgency.

Raleigh stared down at the table as the Queen addressed White. "I understand your concern for the colony that you were appointed to lead, however, as you have certainly been advised, we are at war with Spain. My advisors have informed me that we may be invaded at any moment. All necessary resources are being put aside to address this impending invasion. The destiny of the country rests with our preventing this invasion. Captain Drake is tasked with leading the fleet to confront the Armada, and Sir Walter will lead my ground troops in the event that Captain Drake does not halt the invasion by sea."

She took a short pause in her delivery before she said, "So you see, Mr. White, although the welfare of your colonists are of my deepest concern, the invasion of my sovereign nation is at risk and must take priority."

White looked at Raleigh for assistance in making his case, but it was not forthcoming. Raleigh looked up from the table he had been concentrating while the Queen was speaking, looked him right in the eye and said, "I'm sorry, John, but the Queen is right. We have an obligation to deal with this impending invasion first and before anything else. Now, I would appreciate your retiring to my residence and I'll discuss the colony over dinner with you later this evening."

White stood up, bowed to the Queen and left the room. He had taken transportation to Raleigh's residence and it awaited his return.

When White and Fernandez had sailed away and left Ananias Dare in charge of the colony, he felt very insecure and unequipped to deal with the situation. But after two days of sitting in his cabin grasping with his feelings and discussing the situation with his wife, Elinor, he pulled himself together and began to make plans to move the colony to the mainland. He had in his possession a crude map that his father-in-law, John White, had provided him of the Albemarle Sound and the Alligator River where he was to relocate the colonists.

He had a list of the colonist's names and their occupations. He intended to spread them out at the various five locations and divide the talent freely among the various groups. White had brought back some sample sassafras tress so the colonists would able to recognize them when they saw the trees growing in the wild.

He called the colonists into small groups for about a half hour.

The purpose of these meetings was to brief them, appoint leaders to each group, and explain what was to be expected of them. He emphasized the importance of nurturing the sassafras trees and how they were going to finance their particular little settlements. He informed them that Raleigh had bestowed five hundred acres per man and it was going to be up to each individual colonist to cultivate that land and grow crops as well as sassafras. He also stated that there was an agreement with the Croatoans to teach them to hunt game and they would assist in protecting them from any invading tribe.

After this series of meetings was concluded, everything began to come together. There were three good-size pinnaces at their disposal to transport the cabins to the various sites on the mainland. They estimated that the dismantling of the housing was going to take at least twenty days.

On the seventh day of the dismantling of the cabins, a Croatoan came on the island and informed them that the Puritans on Croatan Island had been forced to move to the mainland by the *weroance* for attempting to convert the natives to their Puritan religion.

Sometime after they moved to the mainland, the Croatoans learn that while the Puritans were building their new homes, a raiding party of Tuscaroras came in the middle of the night and took them prisoner.

"They are being held at a Tuscarora village up at the end of the Neuse River," the Croatoan said.

Ananias had become friendly with one of the Puritans while they were fishing together on several occasions. He felt an obligation to rescue them from the Tuscaroras. Ananias called together the soldiers that were there to guard the colony and asked for volunteers to go with him up to the Tuscarora village and rescue the Puritans.

All of the soldiers volunteered, but it was necessary to have some soldiers remain with the colony for its protection. *If hostile Indian war parties are wandering about, it was imperative that they must be on their guard for the sake of Roanoke Island,* he thought

Four cannons were loaded onto the pinnace along with six soldiers, four crewmen and Ananias, along with the Croatoan who would guide them to the Tuscarora village.

Their destination was sixty miles up the Pamlico Sound to the Neuse River and another ten miles up that river to the Tuscarora village. It was a full two-day trip, and since the wind was coming out of the south, they were required to tack slowing them down even more.

Under normal circumstances when the wind came out of the north where it usually blew, it normally took two days to reach the Neuse River. But with these wind conditions, they didn't reach the mouth of that river for three days.

Ten days prior, the Puritan men had just finished a long day of labor, putting down the foundations for their two cabins. They had a dinner of venison the Croatoans had provided them before they were evicted from the village and were fast asleep by ten o'clock that evening.

Around three o'clock in the morning, a war party of Tuscarora entered the clearing that the Puritans had provided for their cabins. Since the Puritans hadn't begun the construction of their cabins they were forced to sleep in tents. A dog that they had brought with them from the Croatan village began to bark and was suddenly silenced by the Tuscarora warrior.

Before the Puritan men could reach for their harquebuses, they were dragged from their tents and bound tightly. The women were bound accordingly and the four English prisoners were marched away to waiting canoes in the sound.

They were taken up the sound to the Neuse River and then up

the river to the Tuscarora village. They reached the village at about ten o'clock the next morning. It was almost immediately that they realized they were in for some terrible suffering. As they were led through the village, women and children began to strike them with a variety of thin tree branches with thorns at one end.

After being escorted through the crowd of howling Indians, they were taken to a longhouse where the *weroance* greeted them with a look of disgust. He said something to the warriors who had accompanied them, and then they were taken back outside to the waiting crowd.

There were two middle-aged Indian women who took the Puritan women away in different directions. The men were taken to the middle of the village and stripped of all their clothing. And then they were fastened to stakes. Two of the warriors were assigned to guard over them. The Indian children threw stones at the men causing some minor cuts and bruises. Eventually, the warriors chased them off. The Puritan men remained tied to the stakes all day and into the evening.

After dark, a big fire was built in the middle of the village and the whole population of the village circled around the two Puritan men. Two women approached the fire where they took out long sticks that had been burning. At the end of these sticks were red hot sharpened tips. One of the women came up behind one of the Puritan men and placed the hot stick tip between the cheeks of his buttocks. The man screamed and the men and women of the village dissolved in laughter. Another woman burned the other Puritan man in several places all over his body. After they burned the two men without pity, several other Tuscarora women approached and began to cut their flesh with sharp oyster shells. They placed little cuts all over their bodies as the other women continued to burn them. The crowd surrounding the men was delighted with the spectacle.

The crowd parted and a young woman not more that sixteen was seen holding a large sharp English knife. It wasn't clear where she got this instrument, but it was to become apparent that she knew how to use it. She walked right up to one of the pitifully suffering Puritan man and with a big smile on her face showed him the knife. With her left hand, she took his testicles into her hand and with the knife she slowly began to relieve him of them. The pain from this and all the other tortures began to take their toll on this poor suffering individual and within a few minutes he stopped breathing.

The other Puritan man had witnessed his friend's demise and he knew he was about to experience something as diabolical as well from the young woman with the knife. He prepared himself as best he could. He began to pray.

This young Tuscarora woman now turned to the other man and she faced him straight on. She took a moment to look him in his suffering eyes; it was evident that she was going to get a great amount of pleasure from inflicting this torture. She was a true sadist. She reached down and took in her left hand his penis and with the knife in her right hand she began to slowly cut it off. The man's screams could not be heard over the laughter of the crowd. The blood poured forth and ran down his leg. The man lost consciousness and he convulsed. They continued burning him with the pointed sticks until he expired.

The crowd broke into little groups and laughed as they recalled the spectacle they had just witnessed.

After the Puritan women had been forced to watch their husbands being tortured to death, they were dragged away and turned over to the Tuscarora families who claimed them as slaves.

Two weeks after the death of the Puritan men, a pinnace

captained by Ananias Dare, turned slowly into the Neuse River and began its sail west. The soldiers began to prime their harquebuses and the crew readied the cannon.

News of the ship in the Neuse River traveled quickly to the Tuscarora village. A hundred warriors rushed into the woods to prevent the 'pinnace' from appearing in front of the village. About two miles down the river from the village, the warriors saw the ship slowly sailing toward its destination. The warriors readied their bows and each shot a dozen or so arrows in the direction of the ship. Some of these missiles reached their target, but the majority fell into the water a few feet short. One crewman aboard the 'pinnace' was struck in the leg by one of these crudely made arrows, but it didn't penetrate the leather leggings he was wearing.

Ananias had expected an attack before they would reach the Tuscarora village and he had his men at their stations standing by. As soon as the Tuscaroras fired their first volley of arrows, the soldiers took aim with their harquebuses and sprayed the woods along the shoreline. Although the harquebus shot downed several of the braves, the Tuscaroras managed to stand their ground.

Ananias ordered one of the cannons fired into the area where most of the arrows were emanating. The warriors immediately discontinued their aggression and ran through the woods toward their village.

The 'pinnace' continued up the river and dropped anchor with portside facing the Tuscarora village. The population of the village fled into the woods. After a few moments, one of the chiefs of the Tuscarora, Otetiani, came forward and raised his hands indicating that he wanted to talk.

Ananias, escorted by two armed soldiers boarded a jolly boat and went ashore to meet with the chief. They sat on a blanket in the middle of the village as the population peered out from behind the trees in the woods.

The chief attempted to make Ananias understand that the Puritans had been trespassing on Tuscarora sacred grounds and the men were made to pay for breaking Tuscarora law. He informed Ananias that the men were dead, but the women lived.

After a lot of sign language, Ananias made clear to Otetiani, that if the women weren't released immediately, he would destroy the village with his cannon. Otetiani had already seen the destruction the cannon could inflict and he agreed to the release.

After the meeting was concluded, Otetiani disappeared into one of the longhouses while Ananias and his soldiers walked back to the shoreline. Within a few minutes, the two Puritan women came out of the longhouse and began to walk in the direction of Ananias. When the women were in close proximity, Ananias could observe their grief. He put his arms around the women and escorted them into the jolly boat. Once everyone was safely aboard the anchor was aweigh; the ship turned and sailed down the river.

Back in London, the English were convinced that an invasion from the Spanish was imminent and word was received that the Armada was preparing to sail from Spain. Everyone was doing what they could to join in to save England from the aggressive Spanish.

In Spain and throughout Europe, Catholics challenged Queen Elizabeth's right to the throne claiming that Elizabeth was the illegitimate daughter of Henry VIII and Anne Boleyn. They contended that Mary Queen of Scots was the rightful English Queen because she was a legitimate descendant of King Henry VII.

Shortly before John White left for Virginia, Queen Elizabeth's execution of Mary Queen of Scots had exacerbated the antipathy between Queen Elizabeth and Phillip II. With Mary Queen of Scot's death, Philip saw no further reason to delay an attack on England and rid Spain of this troublesome English Queen and her privateers such as Francis Drake.

Thereafter, England was on constant alert for a Spanish attack.

When John White finally met with Raleigh on November 20, 1587, Raleigh was preoccupied with his plantation in Munster, Ireland, and with preparations for the Spanish Armada.

English spies had reported that the Armada was nearly ready to sail. As Vice-Admiral of Cornwall and Devon, Sir Walter Raleigh and his cousin Sir Richard Grenville were responsible for the land defenses of these two countries. Raleigh had little time for White, but he offered a 'pinnace' for immediate relief of the colony. Sir Richard Grenville was already preparing another fleet at Bideford for privateering in the West Indies and installing a military-naval base in Virginia.

Fearing for White's safety at sea, Raleigh instructed White's pinnace to wait several months until Granville's fleet sailed.

In March 1588 as Grenville was ready to sail, orders came down from the Queen's Privy Council to abandon the voyage. The Council ordered Grenville's ships to move to Plymouth and join the fleet awaiting the arrival of the Armada.

White continued pleading for vessels to relieve the colony. After several failed attempts, he finally found two small ships not needed by the Queen in Plymouth. He engaged the thirty-ton bark Brave, and the twenty-five-ton Roe with a crew that included a captive Spanish pilot who knew the waters around the American coast. White took on board fifteen new planter families and supplies for the relief of the colonists.

The two small ships departed from Bideford on April 22, 1588.

Soon after they lost sight of Cornwall, they began to attack any non-English ships they could catch. On May 6, White's bark was itself attacked and boarded by a French ship. The Frenchmen took everything they could transfer to their ship including the Spanish pilot.

White's bark the Brave limped home to England with no weapons or cargo. With no pilot to guide them, the pinnace had no alternative but to go to England without going to Virginia.

As Ananias sailed the pinnace toward Roanoke Island, he spent a considerable amount of time consoling the two Puritan women who were suffering major shock from their experiences with the Tuscarora and witnessing their husbands murdered in such a horrible fashion.

After a full day of sailing, Ananias sat both women down and explained to them what was going to be expected of everyone, including themselves, once all the colonists were resettled on the mainland.

"I expect after a reasonable period of time for you to select another husband from one of the single colonists. There are some very dependable men for you to choose from," he said with a tone of some pity but also determination in his voice.

"But none of the eligible men in the colony are Puritan," one of the women commented.

"My dear lady, what you are going to need when we move to the mainland will be a provider. That is a man who will hunt, plant crops, and keep a roof over your head. A man who will take care of you," Ananias reminded her in a very businesslike manner.

When Ananias and company finally reached Roanoke Island, the colonists had begun to carefully take down the dwellings and was packing the materials for shipping to the mainland.

Ananias made an announcement and informed the colonists of the tragedy that befell the Puritans. He added that the two surviving women had agreed to select a husband from one of the unmarried colonists. They had even agreed to consider taking the Church of England as their religion.

Ananias appointed the five associates who Raleigh had assigned to White to govern the resettlement areas along the Alligator River. As the majority of the colonists were packing and preparing to evacuate the island, Ananias and the five associates boarded a 'pinnace.' And then they sailed to the mainland and down the river. Sites had been identified by White several months earlier, but Ananias wanted these associates to get a first look and be part of any decision that was going to be made.

It took more than four days of walking each of the five areas that had been selected for resettlement, and there was much discussion between these associates. It was agreed among them that each associate would receive a group of colonists who would provide various talents and trades that would guarantee a successful settlement. A settlement of soldiers would guard the mouth of the river and would not allow anyone to pass who could not be identified as English or Croatoan.

When Ananias returned to the island nearly all the dwellings were packed and ready for shipment. The colony only had three pinnaces, so moving all this material was an arduous task. It was estimated that to move and set up on a particular settlement would take nearly six weeks at each site. That didn't include building a palisade, which the settlements would defer erecting until early spring.

The first settlement to be set up was for the soldiers. The soldiers insisted on building a palisade immediately around their living quarters and the placements of their cannons to cover any invaders attempting to break through. This soldier settlement took much longer because of the number of trees that had to be felled and placed into the ground. This alone became a five week project for the initial stage and nearly all winter to finally complete the fort.

As the pinnaces were about to sail to the Alligator River, Ananias called everyone together. The names of the single men were placed in one bowl and the single women were to select names. They were allowed to draw a name and that would be the man they would agree to marry. Morris Allen was the first name chosen by Elizabeth Glane to be her husband. It didn't take very long since there was only eight women and the two Puritan who were not attached in matrimony.

The minister was standing by to marry all the couples that were to be united.

It was agreed that the men who did not obtain a wife through this procedure could take a Croatoan wife when the time was right, or they could wait for more English women to arrive that Raleigh had promised to send later. Croatoan women were attracted to English men and marriages had successfully taken place in the past between these two cultures.

The day before they completely abandoned the island, Margery Harvie gave birth to a little boy. The child was named after his father, Dyonis.

The 119 men, women and children made up the colony. There were eighteen soldiers, five of which were married. The additional eighty-nine English settlers were divided up among the five locations along the Alligator River where over 150 Croatoans were currently living. These Native Americans were going to be valuable in teaching the colonists to hunt and plant crops and fish.

By the late spring 1588, the Roanoke colonists were settled into their new homes along the Alligator River. With a lot of struggle, they had re-erected their homes at the five locations and were working on constructing palisades. In the early spring the women began to plant crops while the men joined the Croatoans hunting.

Ananias was expecting any day to see an English ship sail down the Alligator River loaded with supplies and additional colonists. Sites had already been designated for any new adventurous English who wanted to join their little enterprise.

In the late fall of1588, a Spanish ship slipped through the inlet and made its way down the Pamlico Sound to Roanoke Island to escape a storm. They spotted the palisades on Roanoke Island. The ship dropped anchor and the captain along with two of his officers went ashore. The only thing that remained from the Roanoke Colony was the palisades surrounding a void. It had been obvious that there was once English activity there, but there was no sign of life.

That summer Captain Vicente Gonzalez sailed from St. Augustine. With his thirty soldiers and seamen, he was instructed to find the English colony and destroy it. Spain had been informed by an Irishman, Barbie Glaven, and by spies in Elizabeth's court that an English colony was intended to be established somewhere along the Chesapeake Bay.

Captain Gonzalez had been to the Chesapeake Bay twice before: once on a 1570 expedition to deliver Catholic missionaries and on a 1572 expedition to revenge their massacre. After failing to find Raleigh's colony by a thorough search of the Chesapeake Bay, Gonzalez headed back to St. Augustine with two Indian captives.

Spain reacted to the Gonzalez report by ordering an assembly of a large fleet to eliminate any English they may find in America and to place a fort on the Chesapeake. Instead, however, this order was superseded by another that sent the fleet to Mexico where they received an accumulation of silver, gold and pearls to take to Madrid.

The plan to eliminate the English colony and to settle on the Chesapeake had been Raleigh's overall plan to divert the Spanish away from the English in Virginia. Spanish archives disclose no further attempt to locate the English colony until 1609, when they learned of Jamestown.

Due to the war with Spain that began in 1587, White could not find any ships to take him back to America until 1590. Meanwhile, Raleigh along with his business manager, William Sanderson, organized a holding company for further explorations of Virginia. Sanderson was joined by several wealthy English gentlemen, but no voyages were initiated in 1589. Apparently, Sir Francis Drake had confiscated most of the available merchant ships still heavily armed for Armada defense for an unsuccessful invasion of Portugal. In other words, at that time there were no seaworthy ships for the holding company to send to Virginia.

However, by 1590, a few ships privateering had begun to venture into the West Indies again with and without the Privy Council's permission. A London merchant, one John Watts, had three ships for privateering and ready to sail for the West Indies in June of that year. But their departure had been held up by the general stay that was still in effect from the Queen's Privy Council

White was determined. He saw an opportunity for Raleigh to intercede with the Queen and procure a license for the three John Watts ships to proceed, but only if they agreed to take John White, relief supplies and new settlers with all their necessary furniture to Virginia. Richard Sanderson agreed to add an extra ship to the fleet that would carry everything to the colonists.

Once again when it was time to leave port, the authorities changed their minds and refused to allow the ships to carry passengers or supplies.

White was backed into a corner. He could either go with this small fleet when they sailed or remain and continue to obtain help from Raleigh, who was in Ireland. After weighing the different alternatives, White decided that he must go alone, realizing this might be his last opportunity to get back to the colony, his daughter, and grandchild.

The three ships were the Hopewell, the John Evangelist and the Little John under the Captains William Lane, Abraham Cooke and Christopher Newport. Several years later, in 1607, Captain Newport would transport the Jamestown colonists.

Richard Sanderson's, Moonlight, under Captain Spicer, was left behind by their sudden departure, but caught up with the others in July.

The three ships mentioned left Plymouth about the end of February 1590, and arrived on Roanoke Island in the middle of August. The ships spent all of May, June and July cruising for Spanish ships and attacking Spanish villages around the island of Hispaniola.

They captured a few smaller Spanish ships, but on the May 2, they sighted and chased a fleet of fourteen ships commanded by Vicente Gonzalez who had visited Roanoke Island in 1588.

The Spanish ship Buen Jesus was captured and outfitted to operate with the privateering fleet and the crew was released ashore on the island of Cuba. After a few more unsuccessful chases, two of the ships turned north toward Roanoke Island and the prize ship was sent to England.

On August 12, the fleet anchored off the Croatan Island (Cape Hatteras) to take soundings within the Chacandepeco Inlet. But, after much discussion, it was decided not to visit the island at this time. Three days later they anchored off Port Fernandez and saw smoke rising over the Roanoke Island.

White was optimistic that they would find some of the colonists waiting on the island for his return. On August 16, White went ashore with Captains Cooke and Spicer intending to go to Roanoke. But they saw smoke rising in the southwest by Kendrick Mount and believed they would find some of the colonists there. When they finally reached that area they only found an unattended fire. The search party had wasted an entire day.

On August 17, White once again prepared to go to Roanoke Island, but was delayed by Captain Spicer who had sent his jolly boats ashore for water. Finally, two pinnaces left the Moonlight and approached the inlet. The first pinnace passed over with great difficulty in the rough sea. When the second pinnace attempted to pass it they were upset and Captain Spicer and six crewmen drowned.

The surviving sailors were tempted to give up the search, but eventually were convinced by Captain Cooke and John White to continue. White's party searched for the colonists for the rest of that day and the next.

White wrote in his diary: "*Two boats with nineteen men left Port Fernandez for Roanoke, but it began to get dark. We approached the place where we had left the colonists, but, we over shot the place by a quarter of a mile. A fire could be seen at the north end of the island. After traveling to the site of the fire, we sang English tunes, blew trumpets and called out to the colonists without response. At daybreak, when we finally got ashore, we only found smoldering grass and rotten trees. We turned east and followed the shoreline around the north end of the island until we approached the last place I left the colony. We looked around inside the dilapidated palisade where we noticed footprints of several Indians, perhaps Croatoans on the island for a deer hunt. As I climbed up the sand bank on the last place where I left the colonists, there carved into a tree were the Roman letters 'CRO.' Continuing on to where the houses had been, I found all the houses removed as I had discussed with Ananias Dare. As I walked around the palisade and stood looking at its entrance, carved on a post was the word 'Croatan.'*

CHAPTER VIII

After seeing the message from Ananias, White went down to the shoreline to see if he could find any of the colonists' jolly boats, pinnaces or any weapon that may have been left behind. As he was searching, no boats or weapons were found, but one of the sailors found White's own possessions that he had directed Ananias to bury if the colonists had moved before he returned from England.

The Secotan or the Powhatans had apparently found the chests and most of the contents had been removed. What was left behind was rusted and spoiled. White believed deep in his heart that Ananias had followed his orders and led the colonists to safety on the mainland along the Alligator River.

As they took a moment to reflect on the colony, as storm began to approach. White and the sailors hurried to the ships as the storm became stronger. They reached their ship with difficulty. Captain Cooke sent a boat back for those who had gone ashore to fill their water casks. The men were brought back, but the fresh water had to be left behind.

White swore Captain Cooke to secrecy and confided to him where he believed the colonists were presently located. He didn't, however, give the real reason they had been removed to the Alligator River or anything about the commodity of sassafras that they were cultivating for Raleigh.

After the Captain was informed by White where the colonists had settled, he agreed to take White down the Alligator River in search of them and return later for the water casks that had been left behind.

As the Captain ordered the capstan turned to bring the anchor aweigh, the cable broke and the ship began to move fast toward the shore. With Cooke's good seamanship and the deep channel near the shoreline, they were able to sail around Kendrick Point. But with only one cable and anchor remaining, Cooke would not chance an attempt to pass through the inlet and sail down the Alligator River.

After considerable consultation between White and Cooke, it was agreed that they would sail to San Juan, Puerto Rico or Trinidad for fresh water, food and repairs. They would remain over the winter and seek prizes (Spanish ships), and then the following year they would return to the American coast of Virginia.

The crew of the Moonlight decided not to go south with Cooke. The Moonlight turned for England as Captain Cooke set out for Trinidad. On August 28, another storm forced the Hopewell to lower her sails and run with the wind. As a result, it took them straight in the direction of England. They managed to reach the Azores by September 17, and found the English there in force awaiting the Spanish fleet. Captain Cooke remained with the English fleet until September 30 when he headed for England.

Ananias Dare executed all of the orders of John White after he left the Roanoke Island for England, and he oversaw the establishment of the settlements along the Alligator River one at a time. Everyone worked laboriously and suffered greatly through the winter of 1587 and 1588.

Elinor Dare required several weeks of bed rest due to the massive loss of blood while giving birth to her child, Virginia. She suffered for weeks on end with high fevers and chills. Ananias spent a large amount of time heating irons over a fire and put them in her bed around the clock. Due to Elinor's poor physical condition, Ananias requested Jane Mannering, who had been recently married before leaving the island, if she would look after Elinor and the baby.

Jane Mannering was one of the Puritan women who, not many weeks before, lost her husband under horrific circumstances as described previously. Because of the differences in religious beliefs, Elinor and Jane were not exactly compatible.

Although a complete biography about Elinor Dare has been lost to the ages, we do know that she was born around 1568 in Westminster, London, England and was the daughter of John White. Elinor had had a formal education in London. She was the only child of John White and he sent her to the best schools available. She learned to read and write and studied mathematics.

Elinor and Ananias Dare were married in St. Bride's Church in 1586.

We also know that she left England in the 1587 as part of the Roanoke expedition and was pregnant with Virginia when she boarded the Lion May 8, 1587.

Although Elinor wasn't Puritan, she was more than likely as well as her husband, Ananias, religious separatists. That was one of the explanations why she would leave London and travel to the New World considering her pregnant condition. At that time in England being a religious dissenter could result in a death sentence.

However, Jane took her duties seriously in caring for Elinor and the child Virginia. As time passed, Jane and Elinor became very good friends.

The Croatoan women were also very helpful that first year in their new little colony. Nineteen colonists and twenty-six Croatoans shared the area that had been prepared for Ananias Dare and his family. There were nine houses and two longhouses placed in a circle with a cleared field to the west of the settlement. All the healthy women worked the fields alongside the Croatoan women.

Michael Bishop, one of the single men in the Dare community invited a young Croatoan woman by the name of Gaho to marry him and live in his house. The young woman converted to Christianity before they were married. Many of the young unmarried Englishmen eventually married eligible young Croatoan women and they spent many years teaching each other their different cultures and languages.

It became imperative for the English women as well as the men to learn and adopt the many aspects of the Indian culture in order to survive. Elinor Dare was no different. As the years passed, there would be several times when the survival tricks she learned from the Croatoan women would save her life.

In the 1500s, it was common for the man of the family to instruct his wife in the lessons of his trade. In addition to being a tiler and bricklayer, Ananias was efficient as a stone mason. Whenever someone passed away in the little colony, it was Ananias that was called upon to inscribe a stone with their name, date of birth and date of their demise.

After the little Dare colony was established for about a year and Elinor had regained her health, Ananias spent many hours teaching her his stone mason trade. Elinor was a quick study and Ananias was pleased with her progress. The purpose for these instructions was in the event that anything might happen to him; it would be another way Elinor could earn a living to provide for herself and their child, Virginia.

On one occasion in the fall of 1589, the soldiers at the fort guarding the mouth of the Alligator River saw three canoes with remnants of the Secota and Cotan tribes paddling into the river. The soldiers had previously stretched a chain across the river to prevent any intruders from getting through. At the proper time, the soldiers pulled the chain into a taut position and opened fire on the intended intruders. All the occupants of the canoes were killed and the soldiers confiscated the canoes for their own use.

On another occasion in the spring of 1590, Wanchese, who was now a chief of the Secotan approached the English fort at the mouth of the Alligator River. He requested to speak with the Captain in charge. The Captain feared that it was a trap and refused the invitation. Wanchese was told in no uncertain terms to withdraw immediately or face their cannon. Wanchese and his warriors withdrew without incident.

Between the successful hunting parties between the English and the Croatoan braves, there was always ample meat. The Croatoans had taught the colonists how to cultivate the land for corn and a variety of other vegetables. The plates of the colonists were always full even in the winter. Tons of sassafras was being collected and awaiting the English ships that would bring supplies from England.

In 1590 life was good along the Alligator River and these were five thriving little colonies.

When John White returned back to England for the last time in 1590, he retired to Ireland to write a narrative for Richard Hakluyt. Hakluyt was the Queens historian and spent much of his time promoting colonizing America in the name of the English. Hakluyt presented the Queen and her advisors with his *Discourse of Western Planting*, a sustained and forceful argument for investment in the colonization of the Americas.

Originally intended as confidential counsel, the *Discourse* was not published until the nineteenth century; nevertheless, in addition to Hakluyt's own research, it drew on some information already widely available.

In 21 chapters, Hakluyt argued that colonization would be an ideal opportunity for the English to spread the Protestant faith to Indians and lift the "souls of millions of those wretched people from darkness to light, from falsehood to truth, from idols to the living god, from the deep pit of hell to the highest heavens." He focused primarily, however, on opportunities for the English to exploit the natural resources of the Americas and perhaps reap the kinds of rewards the Spanish had claimed in the West Indies.

While happily dispatching to the new colony the underachievers of England's expanding population, England also would create a needed market for its own goods.

Finally, Hakluyt argued that the Spanish in America were weak—their colonies undermanned and spread too far apart and that allying with the Indians might be enough to destroy their empire.

Hakluyt was responsible for bringing Herriot's account of the Americas, and the related watercolor paintings of Roanoke by John White, to the attention of the Flemish engraver and printer Theodor de Bry. Hakluyt encouraged de Bry to make what originally was a slim pamphlet into a multilingual folio volume, accompanied by de Bry's engravings of Whites illustrations that appeared at the first volume of de Bry's *America* series in 1590. (Hakluyt also translated the illustration captions from Latin into English.) De Bry's edition of "*A brief and true report* " was the product of a remarkable collaboration between Harriot, White, Hakluyt, de Bry, and a number of others, including the famous botanist Charles de l'Ecluse; it made the English colony famous. The illustrations quickly became iconic images of Native Americans.

Beginning in late spring of 1590, Raleigh began sending ships to America. It is theorized that Raleigh knew exactly where to send these ships, collect his sassafras and return to England. Raleigh continued this practice until the death of Queen Elizabeth in 1603.

In 1592, Raleigh displeased the Queen by secretly marrying one of the Queens ladies in waiting, Elizabeth Throckmorton, without her permission. The Queen had both Raleigh and Throckmorton put into the Tower for a year and then banished him to the countryside. Raleigh was allowed to sail to Guiana in 1595, and then return to Elizabeth's court in 1597.

In 1589, the little settlements along the Alligator River were being very productive. Elinor established a close friendship with Margery Harvie who delivered a child a month after Virginia was born. Their children were always with Elinor and Margery as they planted crops, cooked meals and washed their few clothes. They became students of the Croatoan women that lived in their settlement as well.

The men joined with the Croatoan warriors and spent many hours hunting game. Their hunting area was hundreds of square miles that reached all the way up the Chowan River in the west and to the Neuse River in the south. They were sharing this land, no matter how reluctantly, with the Tuscarora in the south, the Weapemeoc Confederation up the Chowan River, and the Secotan on the north side of the Albemarle Sound.

It was a bitter competition, but all the groups exercised restraint during 1589. There seemed to be enough game to go around for everyone. However, time would tell if this restraint could be kept in place if the game became scarce.

In addition to learning cultivation and Indian domestic practices, Elinor was spending a considerable amount of time teaching Virginia to speak and walk. She practiced her stone mason techniques as well and Ananias was proud how Elinor had become a pioneer woman, considering she had been raised in an upper class society and had attended some of the finest schools in England.

In the spring of 1589 an English ship entered the Alligator River. The soldiers raised the chain across the river and forced the craft to drop its anchor. It was a pinnace and was shortly followed by a second one. Since it was flying the English colors, the soldiers didn't unleash their cannons on the craft.

A jolly boat was launched and a captain and his first mate came ashore. They were greeted by the captain of the guard, Charles Florrie.

The captain of the first pinnace presented a letter from Raleigh introducing them. The letter identified them as Captain Richard Arthur and First Mate William Sole. Their ship, the New Bark was anchored just off of Roanoke Island.

The letter from Raleigh stated that these gentlemen were here by permission of the Queen to drop off supplies that had been promised by John White. They were also instructed to pick up "the cargo." The cargo as everyone knew, translated into sassafras.

The two pinnaces were loaded with a variety of goods that included clothing, farming and carpentry tools, ammunition, swords, knives, cooking utensils, pot, pans and medicine. Captain Arthur told the captain of the guard, Charles Florrie, that he would deliver the supplies down the river and when the last of the supplies were finally delivered to the last colony, he would reverse his course and load the pinnaces with the "cargo."

This procedure was agreed upon between the parties and the first 'pinnace' began transferring the supplies destined for the fort.

The next stop for the two pinnaces was the Dare settlement.

When they arrived, Ananias was away on a hunting expedition. Elinor always handled the business transactions of the little colony in the absence of Ananias.

There were clothing items such as warm coats, gloves, shoes and boots, and several fashionable dresses for the young women. Of course, there wasn't anywhere within this crude settlement of houses, longhouses, and muddy streets to wear such apparel, but Elinor was grateful just to have these items just the same.

The Dare colony had collected nearly a thousand pounds of sassafras during the time they lived along the river. When Ananias would go to the old Croatan settlement on the island, he would also bring back from his hunting expeditions bags full of sassafras.

Elinor invited Captain Arthur to dine with her and Margery Harvie whose husband was away with Ananias hunting. She had a thousand questions about what was happening in England.

"Tell me sir, did the Spanish Armada invade England?" Elinor asked.

"The Spanish did the best they could to conquer our sovereign country, but god, the weather and Francis Drake defeated them." He took a pause, bowed his head and said, "God save the Queen!"

Having dinner with this English gentleman was the highlight of the year for Elinor. The life in the colony was difficult and mundane on a day-to-day basis. One of the things that made her life enjoyable living in this little colony was watching her child, Virginia, develop from a baby into a little girl. Elinor's only regret was the child didn't have the opportunities and privileges she had enjoyed as a little girl growing up in England.

Elinor missed her father, John White. She inquired if he knew that the colonists were safely living along the Alligator River and were thriving. Finally, Elinor requested Captain Arthur take a letter to John White from her when he returned to England.

Captain Arthur reminded Elinor that he was in America on a highly secret mission retrieving the sassafras and had to be very careful not to have anyone learn of their existence.

"Raleigh," he said, "wants everyone to believe that the Roanoke Island colony disappeared into the wilderness."

Elinor informed Captain Arthur that she was aware of the necessity to keep their whereabouts secret, it was just she wanted her father to know that they were alive and well following the directions he had left for them in 1587. Elinor drafted a short note and gave it to Captain Arthur for delivery to her father.

Early the next morning, Captain Arthur and his first mate, William Sole, boarded the pinnace and continued down the river to deliver the supplies to the other colonies and to eventually load the cargo for the trip back to England.

Ten days later, and after the New Bark had sailed to England with its cargo, Ananias and Manteo returned to the Dare settlement. Elinor briefed him about the visit from Captain Arthur and showed him the supplies that had been delivered to them. She said that Captain Arthur assured her that Raleigh was going to be sending another ship next year to deliver additional supplies. She assured Ananias that everything her father, John White, had promised was coming to fruition.

Ananias had some distressing news. While the Croatoans and colonists were hunting, they were confronted by a war party of Tuscarora's who threatened them. The Tuscarora's were claiming much of the hunting territory between the Neuse and Pamlico Rivers were their exclusive hunting territory and reminded them that the English and Croatoans were trespassing.

One of the Tuscarora said in a threatening tone, "If you

wander on this land again in the future, we will declare war on your settlements."

Manteo spoke up: "Those lands have always been hunted by my people since the beginning of time. The Tuscarora do not have exclusive rights to those lands. If necessary, my people will fight to protect our hunting rights," he said with indignation.

A few weeks later, word reached the Alligator River that the Secotan had been adopted into the Weapemeoc Confederation. They further learned that their major village had become infected with small pox. The Croatoans told Ananias that the Secotan believed that the English had infected them by some form of magic. The first time the disease had appeared among them was when Harriot had visited the Secotan villages along the banks of the Albemarle Sound.

Harriot in 1585 walked among the Secotan attempting to learn the Algonquian language. He learned that the Secotan believed in the immortality of the soul in a heaven or hell, which was believed to be at the physical end of the earth. Harriot became familiar with some of their priests who became interested in adding the Christian religion to their own.

Harriot said that they were in awe of the navigational instruments, weapons, clocks, and writing tools which the priests assumed the English had been given by the gods. They especially admired the Bible, which Harriot thought represented to them a god as much as any of their idols. Their chief, Wingina, at the time, along with many others, joined the English in prayer and song as they traveled together, and Wingina asked for their prayers when he was twice sick near death.

Fear of offending the English god grew as Harriot and company moved from town to town, and many of the Indians died a few days after they left from the small pox. In contrast, the soldiers that accompanied Harriot appeared to be healthy. They, the Secotan, believed that the disease was a result of some offenses against the English god who punished them through invisible English spirits.

They were having another outbreak of this dreaded disease, probably as a result of poor sanitation practices and keeping clothing worn by Indians who had died in 1585 from the small pox in their houses.

When they would see an English hunting party coming up the Chowan River, they would retreat or fire arrows at the hunters to discourage them from coming near them. The settlements had to be on guard from any potential attacks that might come from the Tuscarora or the Secotan in the future.

Ananias canoed up and down the Alligator River meeting with each leader of the individual colonies and briefing them on the impending danger of Tuscarora and or a Secotan surprise attack. He suggested that every colony fortify their settlement with cannon on the palisade.

He also traveled to the fort at the mouth of the Alligator River and requested that Captain Florrie assign one soldier to every settlement. In addition to the soldiers offering protection to the settlement, Ananias suggested that the soldier train the men of each settlement in the arts of warfare.

It was the fall of the year, 1590, and the settlements began to take the advice of Ananias. Every settlement began to fell more trees to provide material for walkway around the tops of the palisades to position cannon in the event of a raid from hostiles.

The soldiers that were assigned to the settlements began formal classes teaching the boys and women how to care for fire arms and how to use them in an emergency. Elinor learned these lessons well. She knew that someday the colonists may have to use these military instructions to save their lives and the lives of their families.

The winter of 1590 was the harshest since they began living in America. Although it was unusual for it to snow in the Virginia, the climate this year was a punishing winter. The game became scarcer. Ananias, Manteo and the other English and Croatoan hunters avoided the territory between the Neuse and Pamlico Rivers. They didn't want to give the Tuscarora an excuse to declare war.

About halfway through this cold and harsh winter, Ananias and Manteo decided to approach the Tuscarora's for the possibility to trade. The settlements had an ample amount of goods from the delivery of supplies when they were visited by the English ship, the New Bark.

Manteo's wife, Towaye, was a month away from giving birth to their first child. Meanwhile, Ananias and Manteo were trekking across the Croatan peninsula to visit the Tuscarora village. They had taken two Croatoans with them to carry much of the goods that they intended to trade. They were sure that the Tuscarora's would be conducive to trading, since many of the items they were carrying would make life in their village exceedingly better.

About five miles from the village, they met a winter Tuscarora hunting party. At first, the Tuscarora's were suspicious of their presence. Their first impression of Ananias and Manteo was that they were poaching game in their hunting grounds. After Manteo explained to them in their Iroquoian language, and presented to them the quality of goods that had been brought to trade, the hunting party agreed to escort them to their village.

The village was enclosed by a palisade much the same as other Iroquoian tribes across the north. There were no gates, but a very narrow opening where one had to enter before it opened into the interior of the palisade.

When Ananias and Manteo were escorted into the village, a brave had run ahead of the party and alerted the *weroansqua.* As Ananias, Manteo, and their Croatoan friends walked slowly toward the center of the village, they stopped in front of a longhouse that was located on the outer circle of the wigwams.

Ananias expected to see the Tuscarora chief, Otetiani, come out of the longhouse. He was completely overwhelmed with surprise with what he was about to see.

A *weroansqua,* whose name was Dekanawida, pushed aside the animal skin that enclosed the entrance of the longhouse and walked directly to them. Manteo raised his hand in a friendly manner and offered a greeting in her language.

Dekanawida was dressed in a long skirt that was decorated with beads and dyed porcupine quills with leggings. On her top, she wore a deerskin vest and decorative fur cape. She wore her hair in one braid which indicated that she was, or had been at some distant time, married.

Ananias was confused and in a slight form of culture shock. He was not aware that in the Iroquois community, women were the keepers of culture. They were responsible for defining the political, social, spiritual, and economic norms of the tribe. Iroquois society was matrilineal, meaning descent was traced through the mother rather than through the father, as it was in the English culture. While most Iroquois sachems were men, women nominated them and made sure they fulfilled their responsibilities. In this tribe, it was the *weroansqua* who did the trading.

The Tuscarora village was small, but was in keeping with the traditional Iroquoian village layouts. The village was built on high ground and outside the palisade were fields of crops in all stages of growth. Manteo knew that there were probably a large supply of corn, kidney beans, pea beans, squash, pumpkins and melons stored away for their winter. He deduced that there was much more stored than the tribe would need for the winter. Therefore, it was a good bet that the Tuscarora's would be in a mood and position to execute a good trade once they saw the goods that he and Ananias brought with them.

Dekanawida invited Ananias and Manteo to join her in the longhouse. After they entered, they were invited to sit on one of two blankets that were spread out on the floor of the longhouse. Dekanawida sat facing them.

Manteo explained to Dekanawida that they were interested in trading the goods they had brought from their settlement for some deer meat and a variety of crops they had in storage.

"Let me see the goods that you brought to trade," she said in a relatively businesslike manner.

Manteo called out in Algonquian for his Croatoan countrymen who had carried the majority of the goods to the Tuscarora village to bring the goods into the longhouse. The Croatoans set the goods down in front of Dekanawida. After taking a minute to survey everything, she picked up a blanket and felt the texture of the material. There were knives with steel blades and pots and pans made of metal. Large spoons to be used for stirring soup and other foods were inspected by her as well.

Ananias had also brought along the two fashionable dresses that had been given to Elinor Dare by Captain Arthur. Elinor, although she loved those dresses, knew that in practicality they were of little use in the settlement. It was Elinor who suggested taking the dresses to the Tuscarora for trade. She wasn't aware that one of the leaders of the tribe was a woman, but she assumed that if the chief's wife or one of his daughters were to see them a trade would be imminent.

Dekanawida picked up one of the dresses and stood. She held the dress in her front and looked down at the material. She turned and walked in back of one of the animal skins that divided the longhouse. Ananias looked at Manteo and smiled. His smile indicated that they were going to make a trade.

A few minutes later, Dekanawida reappeared from behind the animal skin and stood before Ananias and Manteo wearing the dress. It was obvious she was looking for a compliment on her appearance. Ananias and Manteo simultaneously shook their heads in agreement. The thought occurred to Ananias that Dekanawida at that moment was as beautiful as any English woman he had ever seen.

The trading of goods for food was a success. Dekanawida even offered to have some of her men assist with carrying the food to the first settlement where there would be more English and Croatoan manpower available. She invited Ananias and Manteo to stay the night in the Tuscarora village and to dine with her that evening.

Ananias and Manteo accepted her invitation. Ananias was completely ignorant of the customs and mores of the Tuscarora (Iroquois) culture. Furthermore, although he was aware that this was the same tribe that had kidnapped and tortured the Puritans, he had to deal with these people for the better interest of the settlements.

After the trading had been agreed upon by Dekanawida and the English delegation, Ananias and Manteo were escorted to an empty wigwam and told to wait there until they were summoned to the feast. They were given a drink that had a somewhat intoxicating effect. In other words, they were in good spirits when an Indian maiden summoned them to the feast.

Dekanawida had several women of the tribe prepare a wide variety of vegetables, fruits and meats. More of the intoxicating drink was served. A few of the more important men of the village attended along with Dekanawida's daughters, Otstoch and Waneek.

Several bowls of food were placed in front of the two traders. As the evening passed, the two young women moved into positions next to the guests of honor. Ananias was beginning to feel very uncomfortable having Otstoch sitting so close to him. He eventually excused himself and left to retire in the wigwam that had been assigned to them for the evening.

Manteo on the other hand, enjoyed the company of Waneek. Dekanawida inquired at some point during the evening if he (Manteo) found her daughter agreeable. Manteo was semi-intoxicated and he was truly infatuated with the young woman.

In the Croatoan culture, a warrior was entitled to have more than one wife. In the back of his mind, he knew that his wife, Towaye, was about to present him with a child. He also knew if he brought home another wife, it would be accepted and probably encouraged. Another wife would give Towaye assistance in raising Manteo's child.

During a conversation with Dekanawida, Manteo broached to subject of the capture and torture of the Puritans. Dekanawida said that these people were practicing a form of witchcraft on their ancestor's sacred lands and they had to be punished. Manteo understood the Iroquois culture and could forgive their justification for killing the Puritan men.

The next morning, Ananias, Manteo, and his new wife, Waneek, whom he married the night before, the two Croatoans and eight Iroquois braves left the Tuscarora village and began their arduous trip back to the Croatan peninsula and the Alligator River

The five settlements had temporarily joined to form one due to the harshness of that Virginia winter. About a mile from the settlement the Tuscarora's left the party and began their trip home. Manteo took his new bride directly to his house and introduced her to his other wife, Towaye. Towaye who had just recently delivered a child early was having difficulty performing her domestic duties. It seems that Waneek arrived just in the nick of time.

Trading with the Tuscaroras accomplished two things. First, because of the trade and Manteo taking Waneek as his wife, it established temporarily a peace that would probably last for some time. Secondly, it gave the enlarged settlement enough sustenance to get them through the winter.

When Ananias returned home that cold December day, he was told by one of the soldiers that a lost Powhatan brave in need of food had wandered into the settlement. After he was fed, the Powhatan announced that the chief of his nation was aware that the English had established a settlement on the Alligator River. He was going to send a hundred warriors next winter to launch an attack.

A few days after Ananias and Manteo returned to the settlement, Wenefrid Powell (one of the Puritan women) who had been sharing the house of Ananias and Elinor along with her new husband learned that Manteo had married and returned with a Tuscarora woman. When she further learned that this woman was indeed one of the Tuscarora women that tortured to death her Puritan husband, there was a lot of consternation.

During the next three months, nine adults and three children died of various ailments.

Ananias spent much of the winter making coffins out of hollow tree trucks and with Elinor's assistance, chiseled inscriptions into large stones that were placed over the graves.

Since Elinor had taken up this trade, no one could differentiate a stone chiseled between Ananias and Elinor.

The winter passed slowly, and in April Ananias announced that the planting of crops should get underway. All of the women were expected to participate in the cultivation of the fields.

Ananias and Manteo decided that they should go up the Chowan River, meet with Wanchese, and attempt to enlist his help in the event that the Powhatan invade the colony before the next winter.

Manteo's wife, Towaye, announced that she was pregnant again at the beginning of April. It was about that time, too, that his new wife Waneek announced that she was with child as well.

Ananias and Elinor had spent many hours teaching and playing with their little daughter, Virginia. The child was now almost four years old and very precocious. Ananias and Elinor were very proud of their little daughter and Elinor stated to Ananias:

"One day this little daughter of ours will rule this settlement."

A meeting was held by all of the men in the collective settlement to determine whether or not they wanted to return to their separate settlements or remain in the one where they spent the winter. They had to double and triple up in the living quarters. If they wanted to live and expand the present one, they would have to move their houses to that location.

After much discussion and being aware that they might be attacked by the Powhatans, it was decided that it would be more beneficial if they all lived together. Everyone would pitch in and move the houses. They were going to need all three of their pinnaces to accomplish this move. Ananias and Manteo agreed to use canoes to travel up the Albemarle Sound to the Chowan River for a meeting with Wanchese about the Powhatan problem.

While the majority of the men were moving their houses to the main settlement, Ananias and Manteo began work on a dugout canoe. Manteo was a master at building these kinds of water craft, but in the past when he was living exclusively with his people on Croatan Island, he usually had five or six helpers. It would take several weeks to get it completed and seaworthy.

As a result of their lack of manpower, it was the middle of the summer before the craft was completed and they were ready to leave.

They packed their supplies, (including presents for Wanchese and his wife for the purpose of bribing him into assisting them with protection), and they left the Alligator River and began paddling up the Albemarle Sound.

A few years prior, there had been four Native American villages along the Sound, and now they found all of them abandoned. The remnants of these Secotan people, who now lived with the Weapemeoc Confederation, were gathered together on the upper Chowan River under the leadership of Wanchese. At this point in time, he had about three hundred warriors to send into the field.

Wanchese had spent ten months in England and had shared a room with Manteo in Raleigh's house in London. He was treated very well while he was a guest of the English and it was a mystery to everyone, including Manteo, why he turned on the colonists shortly after his return to America. Manteo was determined to ask him that pointed question when they meet.

CHAPTER IX

As Raleigh sat in his lodgings at the Tower, he continued to concentrate on how to increase his fortune. His surroundings were almost as comfortable as if he were in his home on the Thames. He was allowed to have his wife reside with him. While they were there, she became pregnant with their first child.

Raleigh had displayed on the wall of his Tower lodgings, the crude artist's renderings that White had sketched while he was in America during the second and third trips.

Raleigh had been briefed by White when he returned from the fourth trip to Roanoke Island. He explained to Raleigh that it was evident that Ananias Dare had followed his directions and moved the colonists to the Alligator River. Raleigh had secretly ordered a ship to go to America, drop off supplies and pick up the sassafras that the settlements had collected for him.

Sassafras was just one of many ways that Raleigh added to his fortune.

Sir Water Raleigh was born into a wealthy family; He was the son of a farmer who earned a great deal of money in shipping ventures. Through his father, Raleigh gained an interest in seafaring. Raleigh spent time at Oriel College, Oxford, England before leaving to join the Huguenot army in the French religious war of 1569. Five years in

France saw him safely through two major battles and the massacre of St. Bartholomew's Day, where beginning August 24, 1572 more than seventy thousand French Protestants were killed. By 1576, he was in London as a lodger at the Middle Temple and saw his poems in print. His favorite poetic theme, "the temporary state of all earthly things" was popular with other poets of the Renaissance, a time of great cultural change led by the works of great artists and writers.

After two years in obscurity, Raleigh accompanied his half brother, Sir Humphrey Gilbert, on a voyage apparently in search of a Northwest Passage to the Orient. The voyage quickly developed into a privateering mission against the Spanish. On their return in 1579, Raleigh and Gilbert faced the displeasure of the Privy Council, the advisors to the King. Raleigh's behavior did little to please the council, and he was imprisoned twice in six months for disturbing the peace. Once out of jail, and at the head of a company of soldiers, he sailed to serve in the Irish wars.

Raleigh was extravagant in dress and behavior, handsome, and superbly self-confident, Raleigh rose rapidly at court, which consisted of the royal family and its advisors. His opinion of Ireland was accepted by Queen Elizabeth, and she kept him home as an advisor. He received royal favor as well, including a house in London and two estates in Oxford.

Raleigh was knighted in 1584 and the next year, he became the chief officer of the stannaries (or mines) in Devon and Cornwall, lord lieutenant of Cornwall, and vice admiral of the West. Although he was hated for his arrogance, his reforms of the mining codes made him very popular. He sat for Devonshire in the Parliaments of 1584 and 1586, and then went on to succeed Sir Christopher Hatton as Captain of the Queen's Guard his highest office at court.

In 1582 Humphrey Gilbert had organized a company to settle

English Catholics in the Americas. Although forbidden by Elizabeth to accompany his half brother, Raleigh invested money and a ship of his own design to the mission. After Gilbert's death on the return from Newfoundland, a region that is now a province of eastern Canada, Raleigh was given a charter to occupy and enjoy new lands. Raleigh sailed as soon as he had his charter and reached the Carolina shore of America, claiming the land for himself.

At the same time, Raleigh sought to persuade Elizabeth into a more active role in his proposed colonizing venture, which would settle lands newly discovered in America. Although unconvinced, the Queen reluctantly gave a ship and some funds. Raleigh remained at court and devoted his energies to financing the operation. The first settlers were transported by Raleigh's cousin, Sir Richard Grenville. Fights, lack of discipline, and hostile Indians led colonists to return to England with Francis Drake in 1586, bringing with them potatoes and tobacco—two things that were unknown in Europe until that time.

John White led a second expedition the next year. The coming of the Spanish Armada delayed the sending of supplies back to the colony for more than two years. When the relief ships reached the colony in 1590, it was reported to have vanished. Later, Raleigh sent other expeditions to the Virginia coast but failed to establish a permanent settlement there. His charter would eventually be withdrawn after Queen Elizabeth's death in 1603.

John White visited Raleigh while he was in the Tower. He told White that he was planning to send two of his own ships to resupply the colonists on the Alligator River. Raleigh suggested to him to write a letter to his daughter, Elinor.

As agreed, this would be a secret mission and was not to be mentioned to anyone. Raleigh also agreed to funnel some of the funds derived from the sale of the sassafras to him.

It was the spring of 1590; some English ships were now allowed to carry on commercial activity once again since the Spanish Armada had been defeated. White watched with anxiety as the two ships Raleigh told him were headed for America and would have contact with his daughter, Elinor, sat at the harbor.

The ships were sitting side by side in the Plymouth harbor. The Hope was being captained by Ambrose Lawrence and the Duyfken by Clement Sutton. Both of these men had seen action under Francis Drake while fighting against the Armada in 1588.

As Captain Lawrence walked down the pier to board a jolly boat, White approached him. "Sir, I am an acquaintance of Sir Walter Raleigh. He agreed to allow me to have a brief word with you. I am familiar with your destination and I have a letter for delivery to one Elinor Dare. Please tell her that I think of her every day and she's in my prayers," he said as he passed the sealed letter to Captain Lawrence.

Captain Lawrence took the letter and put it on the inside of his coat. And then he boarded the jolly boat to be taken to the waiting ship. John White slowly walked back to his lodgings that overlooked the harbor.

The next morning at seven o'clock, White looked out his window of his lodging as both of the ships, the Hope and the Duyfken aweigh their anchors and raised their top sails. He watched as the two ships and their four pinnaces drifted out of the harbor in a straight line and into the English Channel.

John White's heart was heavy for he knew that he may never see his beloved daughter Elinor again. He packed his suitcase and booked transportation back to Ireland.

Captains Lawrence and Sutton were not botanists, but they had been instructed by Raleigh when they had visited him at the Tower three days before. Raleigh educated them about the production of sassafras and how to identify it.

Raleigh told them the following: "Once the leaves bud out in the spring, they remain green through the summer and early fall. The oval leaves grow four to eight-inches and two to four-inches wide. The fall of the year is the best time to harvest the leaves." He took a slight pause to ensure that they were paying attention.

"Therefore, when you arrive in America you will go directly to Roanoke Island, anchor your ships in the little harbor and send the pinnaces to the Alligator River. There you can deliver the supplies to the colonists, collect all the sassafras they have collected and assist them with the fall harvest of that valuable leaf," Raleigh said.

Three days out the ships were hit by an Atlantic summer storm. The ships managed to remain together, but two of the pinnaces were damaged.

Since they were in close proximity to Sao Miguel and Porta Delgada, they stopped there for repairs. As usual the Portuguese delegation came out to the lead ship, the Hope. Captain Sutton came over to the Hope on a jolly boat for the meeting. The Portuguese wanted to know their business on the island. They were shown the pinnaces and the damage they experienced during the storm.

The Portuguese told them that a drydock facility was at their disposal. All in all, it would set the expedition back a week or more for the repairs.

During that time they would replenish their water supply and purchase food from the local vendors. The captains had time to meet with the pilot and study the charts that were given to them by Raleigh before they departed England.

The charts consisted of sketches made by John White on his two tours of the Outer Banks, the Roanoke Island, the Pamlico

Sound, the Albemarle Sound, the Pamlico River and the Neuse River. Soundings in all of these locations were made by Fernandez and were indicated on the charts.

Another chart of the Alligator River and approximate locations of groups of colonists was also provided.

The ten days the two pinnaces were in drydock passed slowly, but turned out to be productive. Fresh water was obtained and brought aboard the ships and food supplies were purchased from the Portuguese vendors.

On August 2, the Hope and the Duyfken, followed by their four pinnaces, raised their anchors and sailed out of Porta Delgada. There was another fifteen hundred miles of open ocean between themselves and the Outer Banks of Virginia.

Meanwhile back in England, Raleigh in his quarters at the Tower met with Samuel Mace who captained a twenty-ton ship called the Vanguard. He provided Mace with a chart of the Outer Banks and identified the Croatan Island (Hatteras). He also shared with him the abundance of sassafras trees reported to exist there. He agreed to share with him the profits of any product he would return to England.

With charts provided by Raleigh of the Outer Banks, Mace sailed in three days after their meeting. About the same time, there were two ships captains preparing to leave Weymouth Port for an unauthorized voyage to the Northern Part of Virginia (New England) for the purpose of establishing a fur trading post.

The captains in question were Bartholomew Gosnold and Bartholomew Gilbert in their ships the Michael and Elizabeth Jonas and they reached the island of Bermuda six weeks later. It was midsummer and the ships were showing signs of worm infestation. They beached the two ships and began replacing the damaged wood.

This was a laborious project and it took several weeks. By the time everything was completed and they were ready to continue on their way, it was the middle of August.

When the two ships reached the American coast, they anchored off of Cape Cod. As they were erecting housing for the crew, Captain Gosnold noticed something that was as valuable as finding gold, there were sassafras trees everywhere.

All activity other than collecting the sassafras leaves was put on hold. They filled the holds of the ships with bundles of leaves and when they couldn't find space for any more of the product, they even stored a goodly amount in their cabins.

They sailed immediately for their home port, Weymouth.

It was mid-November when they arrived home. As luck would have it, Samuel Mace had arrived the day before with a ship load of sassafras from the island of Croatan. Raleigh had been released from the Tower and had come to Weymouth port to meet with Mace. When he saw the two ships, the Michael and Elizabeth Jonas arriving, and when he learned that they had just returned from Virginia without authorization, he had the cargo confiscated for violating his charter rights. Raleigh was concerned that this new supply of sassafras would lower the price on the English market. He also realized that discovery of sassafras elsewhere in Virginia threatened his monopoly. In a letter to Sir Robert Cecil, Raleigh asked Sir Robert to help maintain his charter rights.

Although Raleigh knew the approximate location of the supposed missing colonists, which was based on the information provided to him by John White, he composed a letter to Sir Robert Cecil. Raleigh repeated the claim that the fate of the missing colonists was not known. The colonists and their location were going to be his sassafras factory and he wanted to ensure that it was a guarded secret.

Eventually, Raleigh realized that other merchant seamen, much like Gosnold and Gilbert had at Cape Cod could impact his sassafras industry as well. He took steps to minimize this impact.

He sent his share of the sassafras cargo to Germany to keep it off the English market. Because Gilbert was well connected in Court, Raleigh decided to negotiate a deal with him. He allowed Gilbert and his associates to keep part of their sassafras. In return, Raleigh required that the brief relation written by John Brereton be submitted to him for editing before its release.

The authorized voyage of Samuel Mace was described by John Brereton in his *Brief and True Relations* added an addendum to his report—very likely at Raleigh's insistence. The following addendum gave Raleigh's rationalization for the failure of his ships to find the abandoned colonists and, in this manner, continued to hide their location:

This is a brief Note of sending another bark this present year, 1590, by the honorable knight, Sir Walter Raleigh, for searching out of his Colony in Virginia. Samuel Mace of Weymouth, a very sufficient mariner and honest sober man and who had been to Virginia twice before, was employed by Sir Walter Raleigh to find those people which were left there in the year 1587. Unfortunately, no trace of these people was found.

Brereton's addendum disclosed that Raleigh had sent six voyages in search of those left behind in Virginia in 1587. Although, Raleigh's claims that no trace of the colonists were found, all of the voyages returned large quantities of sassafras.

On August 16, the Hope and Duyfken saw land appear on the horizon. The pilot noticed a patch of land jetting out into the ocean which he identified as Croatan Island. He was aware that, according to the charts he had in front of him, the inlet near the island was hazardous and shallow. This was the inlet that Fernandez ran the Tiger aground and ruined the majority of the supplies for the second voyage.

The pilot had the ship turn to the north and sail up the Outer Banks until they saw another inlet. They dropped anchor's about one hundred yards off the beach and launched a jolly boat to take soundings. When the jolly boat reached the inlet, it became obvious that the tide was coming in and, according to Fernandez's soundings on the charts this was an ideal time to sail into Pamlico Sound.

Both ships aweigh anchors and in a short period of time were sailing for Roanoke Island, which could be seen on the horizon. Two hours later, the two ships and the 'pinnaces' entered the little bay off the northeastern side of the island and dropped anchors.

They unloaded some supplies and pitched tents within the abandoned stockade. Since it was getting dark, they built a fire and prepared food for the crew. They bedded down for the night on the island.

Next morning, supplies and trading goods were loaded into the pinnaces and following John White's charts and written directions, the pinnace sailed around the island and into the Albemarle Sound.

After sailing about ten miles up the sound, the mouth of the Alligator River opened before them. They made a gentle turn and began sailing down the river. Not more than a mile from the mouth of the river, they were ordered to stop and be boarded. Four soldiers, heavily armed, approached the pinnaces in a jolly boat. They demanded to speak to the person in charge of the flotilla. The first mate of the Hope stepped forward.

"I am here on a mission for Sir Walter Raleigh and with the knowledge of John White," he said. He handed a letter from Raleigh acknowledging their legitimacy.

"It is good to see you. We've been expecting you for about a month," the soldier said as he handed the letter back to the first mate.

"We're sorry for the delay, but a storm damaged two of our ships and we had to pull into an island port halfway here for repairs," the soldier was informed.

"We will escort you to the settlement. They are expecting you," the soldier said as he climbed back into the jolly boat.

They sailed on down the river followed by the jolly boat. As they came to a slight turn in the river the settlement came into view. There were several dozen houses lined up next to and facing one another. There were two longhouses at the far end of the street. The street had been named by the colonists White Street, after John White their original leader.

As the pinnaces grounded at the shoreline the colonists surrounded these new comers from England. They immediately entered into conversation asking questions about the state of things in England since they'd left.

The First Mate called out for Elinor Dare. As she stepped forward, he handed her the letter that John White had requested Captain Lawrence to deliver. Elinor took the letter and when she saw who it was from she held it close to her heart for a few minutes before opening it.

As she read the letter she began to cry. It was later learned; when she revealed the letter's content to Ananias after he returned from his mission with Manteo, that her father was intent on coming back to America and promised take her little family back to England. He had been negotiating with Raleigh for a ship.

The crews of the pinnaces began passing out the supplies to the colonists and loading the packaged sassafras leaves into the pinnaces. The sassafras trees were now in full bloom. With the help of the colonists, they began to attack the trees relieving them of all their leaves.

At the beginning of the summer, Manteo's wives had left the settlement due to the harassment from the previous Puritan wives and took up residence in one of the old settlements. Two of the pinnaces disembarked from the main settlement and sailed down the river to visit Manteo and his family.

After they spent a considerable amount of time collecting sassafras leaves along the river, they finally arrived at the settlement where Manteo's two wives were reported to be living. But the occupants were gone. There wasn't any sign of struggle and their dwelling was undisturbed. The men in the pinnaces spent a few hours collecting sassafras leaves around the clearing, boarded the pinnaces and sailed back up the river.

When they finally arrived back at the settlement there was a big feast in their honor with the settlers. Early the next morning the pinnaces began their trip back up the river and a rendezvous with the larger ships.

When Ananias and Manteo arrived at Waratan, the capital village of the Weapemeoc Confederation, the warriors didn't attack them but they were treated with suspicion. As they were escorted to the center of the village, Wanchese stepped toward Manteo and greeted him like a long lost brother. They had spent ten months living together in London and had developed a close bond. Wanchese didn't know Ananias, but extended his hand in a sign of friendship. Led by Wanchese, they retired to a longhouse for refreshments and conversation.

Eventually, Ananias confronted Wanchese with the information they had extracted from a Powhatan scout who had come to their settlement in search of food. The scout had told them that the chief of the Powhatans had ordered a hundred warriors to prepare for an invasion of the settlements along the Alligator River. The scout had further told them that the invasion would probably take place during the winter months when the settlers would least expect it. It was learned later that this bit of information was misleading.

Wanchese sat and listened to Ananias describe the pending invasion by the Powhatans.

He took a slight pause and then he said, "It is true that Wahunsunacock [Powhatan] is capable of having his warriors launch such an invasion. Word has reached the Powhatan how the English has wiped out and crippled many of the Indian tribes to the south," Wanchese said.

Wanchese took a pause and then he said, "Powhatan has decided that before the English grow in strength, it would be better to attack them now while they are still weak."

A silence fell over the conversation. Manteo was very blunt in his next question. "Why we came here, my brother, was to request your help in the event the Powhatan launch an attack on us."

Wanchese looked at Manteo and his response surprised him as well as Ananias. "The immediate threat to your settlement is not from the Powhatan who are hundreds of miles away, but from your neighbors on the Neuse River, the Tuscarora. The war drums are beating in that village."

Manteo and Ananias looked at each other in wonderment. Since Manteo had taken the daughter of the Tuscarora *weroansqua*, it was believed that peace existed between the two peoples. What Manteo and Ananias hadn't taken into consideration was the drought and how it has affected the lack of game of the Croatan Peninsula. The Tuscarora and the colonists were in competition for the few remaining game left.

"I would suggest to you my brother to move your family here at once before the settlement where you now live is attacked," he offered.

"And what do you suggest that we do with the rest of the colonists," Ananias questioned.

"I wasn't inviting you. You are the leader of the colonists and must stay with them though this war with the Tuscarora," he said.

At that point the conversation came to an end. They were offered some refreshments and stood to leave. Ananias felt a sick feeling come over him. He knew that the trip here was a failure. The Secotan were not going to offer their assistance. It became obvious that Wanchese and the surviving Secotan who now live with the Weapemeoc hadn't forgotten about the killing of their chief, Pemisopan, and he didn't trust the English. He was extending to Manteo and his family refuge from the impending invasion of the Tuscarora but not the English.

Manteo thanked him for his offer, but said that he had made a commitment to the English settlement and would honor that commitment. Wanchese walked with them to where their canoe was beached and watched as they slowly drifted down the Chowan River and into the Albemarle Sound.

Back in England, John White was patiently waiting for a ship that Raleigh had promised him to come to fruition. As he sat eating his dinner at a tavern in the seaport town of Weymouth, he suddenly felt a sharp pain envelop his chest. With both his hands, he grasped his chest and collapsed onto the floor. By the time two of the patrons reached White, it was obvious that he was dead.

When word reached Raleigh of John White's demise, he immediately redirected the ship that he was going to be given to White for the rescue his daughter, Elinor, and had it added to the fleet of five ships that he was planning to send to Virginia to collect sassafras. They had no plans to visit the settlement. Raleigh didn't want to have the expense of providing supplies and trading goods to this expedition.

As the colonists were hunting on the Croatan Peninsula that fall, nine colonists were ambushed by Tuscarora warriors, three of the colonists were killed and two more wounded. When they arrived back at the settlement they raised the alarm. They secured the stockade and soldiers were sent for from the little fort at the mouth of the river. Two soldiers were left at the fort manning the cannons and twenty-two soldiers armed with harquebuses were sent immediately to the settlement.

It took Manteo and Ananias twelve hours to reach the Alligator River and another hour and a half to finally reach the settlement. Since they had been made aware of a pending attack by the Tuscarora through Wanchese, they were on alert.

When they reached the settlement, the soldiers had already put the settlement stockade on military alert and all of the men over the age of sixteen were issued firearms. There was another hunting party somewhere on the Croatan Peninsula and the settlement was concerned for their safety.

Shortly after Manteo and Ananias returned, the hunting party came up the river in their canoes. They had been warned by gun shots from the ambushed hunters who were located about a half mile away. When they moved in the direction of the shots, they saw a Tuscarora war party moving through the woods near the river. As the war party passed, one of the Croatoans with them overheard a Tuscarora warrior mention the attack on the other hunting party. They fled to their canoes and paddled back to the settlement.

When Ananias and Manteo arrived back at the settlement, they learned that Towaye had returned to the settlement. She told the colonists that she had been captured by a Tuscarora hunting party who killed her baby. She was in captivity for three weeks and she constantly looked for ways to escape.

One night as they were camped, the Tuscarora warrior standing guard fell asleep. Towaye was very familiar with the geography of the Croatan Peninsula; she slipped away and spent two days making her way back to the settlement. She also added that Waneek, Manteo's Tuscarora wife had decided to return to her people and took their child as well.

Ananias, Manteo, the men of the settlement and the captain of the soldiers had a conference as to what they should do. After several hours of discussion, they were divided as to what action they should take.

Ananias was confident that Manteo could convince Wanchese to allow the colonists to settle near them along the Chowan River. He argued that the Tuscarora would more than likely not follow them there. They were at peace at this time with the Secotan and secondly, their main objective was to take complete control of the Croatan Peninsula for hunting purposes. There were twelve colonists and ten Croatoans that decided to follow Ananias; the rest of the colonists and Croatoans were determined to stay along the Alligator River and take their chances and defend their settlement.

Manteo said that he would travel ahead of the colonists and impose on his friendship with Wanchese to accept those colonists who wanted to relocate somewhere along the Chowan River. Wanchese was now the chief of the Secotan. Manteo believed that Wanchese could convince his people that it would be advantageous to be aligned with the English and what they (the English) could offer to them in trade.

Manteo and Towaye left ahead of the colonists for the Chowan River and a meeting with Wanchese to negotiate for a settlement.

The colonists that had decided to leave with Ananias stripped everything out of their houses, gathered as much of the crops as they could store in baskets and began to load one of the pinnaces. Once all of the colonists that were leaving with Ananias got into canoes four at time, Ananias would lead the flotilla, sailing the pinnace up the Alligator and into the Albemarle Sound.

The first day they only made about half the distance to their destination. They camped on the south side of the sound and the soldiers posted sentries to watch over the colonists. Early the second day, and before they continued their journey, Manteo and Towaye arrived at their camp. He informed Ananias that he had a long meeting with Wanchese, called on his previous friendship and reminded him how he was treated by the English when he was their guest while visiting England. Wanchese reluctantly agreed to allow the English to settle near his village.

They reached the head of the sound by mid afternoon and turned into the Chowan River. Manteo had them stop there until he approached Wanchese to learn where the colonists could set up a settlement.

Wanchese wasn't surprised under the circumstances that some of the colonists had evacuated the settlement on the Alligator River. He knew the Tuscarora had over five hundred warriors at their disposal and would not hesitate in using all of them.

Manteo had previously explained to Wanchese that the colonists were not asking for the Secotan protection, they just wanted to escape the wrath of the Tuscarora and live in peace.

Wanchese said that there was good land on a small creek not far from his village where the fishing was especially good and the soil was fertile. If they wished to hunt, they must go into the woods several miles to the north and away from land where the Secotan have reserved for their hunting grounds.

Manteo agreed with Wanchese conditions.

Manteo went back to where Ananias and the colonists were waiting and explained the details of his meeting with Wanchese.

Manteo led them to the area on the small creek (present day Salmon Creek) that had been designated for them by Wanchese. It was now late in the fall of the year. Hopefully, the winter would not be as harsh as it was in 1590.

They began immediately to fell trees to build a habitat for the individual families. The colonists worked well together and had a lot of experience working with wood and constructing houses. The first thing they built was something that resembled an Indian longhouse. They were capable of building one of these structures in a day. After ten days, they had three longhouses built and it was going to provide shelter for entire group for the winter. They planned in the spring to begin construction on permanent English-type houses.

On the second evening in their new home, Elinor had a long talk with her husband. She informed him that if her father returned at some point as he had originally promised, it was her intention to return to England with him.

Of course, she had no way of knowing that John White had died. But still, she held out hope. She didn't want to continue living in America under these harsh conditions. She also wanted her daughter to go to an English school and become a refined young lady.

The colonist men, as soon as the longhouses were completed, planned to go hunting to the north of where they were camped. Manteo requested from Wanchese two of his braves to escort them as guides. Manteo managed to develop a rapport with these braves and they were very helpful in leading the party to the best hunting areas. On the first day, they managed to locate a herd of deer and they killed five. The second day was a repeat of the first. There were now over twenty-six mouths to feed and without a harvest it was going to be difficult getting through the winter. The colonist men were going to be required to hunt every day.

While they were out with the Secotan guides, they marked trees along the way to aid them in finding their way in this new landscape if they hunted alone in the future. After a short period of time, the colonists became very familiar with these new woods and felt quite at home.

As the winter months passed, the colonists began making plans for the spring. The winter of 1590 and 1591 was milder than the winter before and they were able to clear land for planting in the spring. The men were having more than unusual luck with hunting and in addition to killing deer they managed to bag a number of duck and pheasant. Wild turkey was also plentiful.

They had even identified hundreds of sassafras trees growing wild around their settlement. At some point, one of the colonists suggested that one or more of the men should take a canoe, paddle down the sound to the island of Roanoke, and leave another message on a tree letting any of Raleigh's ships that would be coming to pick up a cargo of sassafras of their new location. On the other hand, it was decided not to pursue that suggestion. They didn't want anyone, especially the Spanish to know of their location.

Everything was coming together back at the colony on the Alligator River. In the early spring, the colonists were beginning to plant crops and the hunting was especially good. These colonists were looking forward to a prosperous and peaceful summer. They had been led to believe that the Powhatans would not attack them until the winter if at all.

Their optimism and false sense of security for the future was ill advised. There was a deadly cloud in the form of Powhatan warriors heading in their direction for the purpose of war.

CHAPTER X

As the colonists along the Alligator River went about their daily activities during that early spring of 1590, they anticipated that a war party from the Powhatan tribe was on a mission to kill them, so they were anticipating an attack.

In the late summer 1589, at the Powhatan village of Werewocomoco along the York River, their chief, Wahunsunacock, had heard about these English from the Roanoke who had migrated north. Wahunsunacock learned that colonists had raided and wiped out several Indian villages along the Albemarle Sound. These white men from across the ocean were also intruding on his domain by sailing into the Chesapeake Bay and making contact with his subjects. To make matters worse, they made no effort to pay tribute to him after making these contacts. As far as Wahunsunacock was concerned, they were not playing by his rules and were a threat to the Powhatan kingdom.

The Powhatan Confederacy was made up of at least thirty Algonquian-speaking tribes that occupied the coasts of Virginia and Chesapeake Bay. The major Indian tribes in the confederacy besides the Powhatan were the Arrohateck, the Appamattuck, the Pamunkey, the Chickahominy, and the Mattopony

The tribes of this confederacy gave mutual military support, as well as paid taxes to Powhatan in the form of food, animal furs, copper, and pearls. There were at least two hundred settlements in the region, many of which were fortified by palisades. The villages were near cultivated fields where the women farmed corn, beans, squash, and other vegetables. The men focused on hunting, fishing, and warfare.

The Powhatan Confederacy had been at war with all the Iroquoian-speaking tribes for hundreds of years. Since the English now lived in close proximity with the Tuscarora, and since the Tuscarora were an Iroquoian tribe, this temporarily would have the Tuscarora's support of the settlements if the Powhatan were to invade this area of the Pamlico Sound.

The Croatan for years had lived peacefully with the Tuscarora and even helped each other in times of need. The Croatan knew as well that if the Tuscarora learned the Pamlico Sound was to be attacked by the Powhatan, they would consider that invasion against them.

The Tuscarora were a very powerful tribe in Virginia. They had established large villages along the Neuse, the Tar and the Pamlico Rivers. They called their main village Chattoka and were located at the head of the Neuse River where the city of New Bern is located today.

The settlement leader, now that Ananias had moved west, was Dyonis Harvie, husband of Margery and mother to the other English child born in America, Emme.

Dyonis asked two Croatoan brothers, Rowtag and Wematin to go to the Tuscarora village up the Neuse River and inform them of the pending invasion by the Powhatan. The brothers were to offer a proposition to the Tuscarora that they and the colonists along the Alligator River could combine forces to meet and defeat the Powhatan invaders when they came south.

Rowtag and Wematin had visited the Tuscarora village several times before when they hunted with them and had learned their language. Over the years, they had even bonded with several of the Tuscarora warriors.

As they left the settlement, the colonists were optimistic that the Tuscarora would be more concerned about a Powhatan invasion than any intrusion of the English along the Alligator River.

Powhatan had sent word to ten of the villages and ordered them to provide ten of their best warriors for this crusade. The Powhatan plan was for the warriors (one hundred in all) to congregate at the village of Chesepian under the leadership of a young Powhatan warrior named Ahanu.

Once the ten warriors of the various villages arrived, they were instructed by Ahanu on his plan of attack. Powhatans in war were very straight forward. Through their scouts, the Powhatans were made aware that the Roanoke Island was uninhabited at this time. They intended to move onto the island and use it as a command center with which to launch their attacks.

They had been told by a Secotan warrior several months before, that there was a settlement of English and Croatan along the Alligator River, and another smaller group camped on the Chowan River at the head waters of the Albemarle Sound. What they didn't have factored into their plan was the fact that the Tuscarora along the Neuse River were considering this incursion as an attack on their home land.

About two hundred Tuscarora warriors were committed to march toward the settlement along the Alligator River to meet the Powhatans head on if they were to invade. Neither side knew where this battle was going to be fought, but they were going to be on a collision course.

The Powhatan plan under Ahanu was to canoe down from Chesapeake past the mouth of the James River and into the Atlantic Ocean. All the while the Powhatans would keep close to the land until they reached the Outer Banks. Once they saw the water of the Pamlico Sound, they would come ashore at the Outer Banks and carry their canoes until they could eventually launch them into the sound. They would then canoe down the sound to the island. When they arrived near Roanoke Island, they would send a few warriors ashore to ensure that it was not occupied. After they were satisfied the island was uninhabited, they would go ashore and make camp.

Two months before in England, Raleigh had sent five ships to America for the sole purpose of gathering and returning to England his beloved sassafras. Almost immediately, he came under criticism for not doing enough to locate the "Lost Colony." Of course, Raleigh knew the colony was not lost, and furthermore he knew their exact location. He wasn't aware that Ananias and some of the colonists had moved to the Chowan River to the west, but he didn't have any intention to bring any of them home. For public relations purposes, Raleigh advertised that he was sending a ship with the specific intention of finding the "Lost Colonists" and bringing them home to England.

He commissioned Captain Samuel Mace to sail the newly acquired, decommissioned British Navy ship, Ayde. She was equipped with eighteen guns and had previously did battle with the Spanish Armada in 1588. Mace was told by Raleigh to spread the word that the Ayde was going on a recovery mission, but of course the real mission was to find and return to England, sassafras.

Mace had aboard as his pilot scientist-navigator Thomas Harriot. Harriot was with John White on the second trip to Virginia. Harriot and White had documented and mapped much of the

Pamlico Sound and its rivers.

After two and a half months at sea, the Ayde reached the shoreline of the Outer Banks, and Harriot guided the ship through the inlet without any difficulty. He suggested to Mace that they sail to Roanoke Island and let the pinnace they had brought along sail up the Albemarle Sound to the Alligator River and down to the settlement. He assured Mace that they would procure a cargo of sassafras there.

What Mace and Harriot weren't aware was that the Powhatan had already reached the island and had set up camp. As they sailed north down the sound toward the island, a canoe of Powhatan was spotted moving in their direction.

As the canoe approached within shouting distance, Harriot called out to them in Algonquian. They shot four or five arrows in his direction nearly hitting him. He scurried to the opposite side of the ship for cover. Two of the soldiers who had witnessed the aggression opened fire with their harquebus killing the two Powhatans who had fired the arrows. The two Powhatans who had been rowing raised their hands in the fashion of surrender.

After the two Powhatans were brought aboard Harriot began to question them. The warriors told Harriot that they had been sent by their chief, Wahunsunacock, to evict the English from his territory. The Powhatans told Harriot that there were a hundred warriors that came down the coast yesterday and were camped on Roanoke Island. Their plans were to go up the Albemarle Sound, find the English settlers and kill them.

After Harriot translated to Mace what the Powhatans told him, Mace invited Harriot into his cabin for a private conversation.

Mace offered Harriot a glass of wine and had him sit down at a table across from him. "Mr. Harriot," he said. "My orders from Sir

Walter were very specific. I was to come to America for one specific reason: to gather aromatic woods, plants, and especially sassafras. Sir Walter was adamant that we were not to have contact with the colonists that he sent here in 1587. First of all our ship is not transporting supplies to those people. Sir Walter has decided that supporting that settlement up the Alligator River is now over. He believes that he can get all the sassafras he wants by just sending ships like mine here, collecting it, and transporting it back to England."

Mace took a slight pause and then he said, "John White is dead. He was the only reason that Sir Walter continued to supply those people. As far as Sir Walter is concerned, the colonists are dead. He doesn't want our crew when we arrive back to England circulating rumors about their whereabouts. I am going to release the two Powhatans on deck and let the warriors on Roanoke Island deal with those colonists."

Harriot got a sick feeling in his stomach. He knew several of the colonists and believed if the circumstances were different, he could have been one of those people abandoned by Raleigh in this foreign land.

The two men had another glass of wine and walked back onto the deck. Harriot told the two Powhatans that they were free to go. The crew assisted them off the ship and back into their canoes.

As the two Powhatans paddled back toward Roanoke Island, Mace had the Ayde turned south in the direction of Croatan Island. They stopped several times along the shoreline of the mainland and had the crew go ashore and collect sassafras.

They finally landed on the island of Croatan. There were still several families of Croatoans living there and they welcomed the English in their usual friendly manner.

Mace, Harriot, and the crew spent the next two weeks collecting sassafras until the hole of the Ayde was overflowing with sassafras cargo.

They bid their Croatoan hosts farewell, aweigh the anchor of the Ayde, unfurled the sails and began the voyage back to England.

Back on Roanoke Island, the lead warrior of the Powhatan war party, Ahanu, brought all the braves together for a plan of action. He decided that instead of attacking the settlement from the Alligator River, he would have the warriors paddle over to the mainland and make their way through the woods to surround the settlement.

When the Powhatans landed on Roanoke Island, there had been several Croatoans living there. Before the Powhatans could capture them, they had escaped to the mainland.

He was sure by now that the colonists had been made aware of their purpose and presence, so the element of surprise was not going to be an option.

Early the next morning, ninety of the Powhatan warriors paddled in their canoes to the mainland. The remainder of the Powhatans remained on the island to ensure that their escape route would not be cut off.

The Powhatan warriors trudged through the swampy landscape of the Croatan peninsula most of the day until they reached the opposite shore of the Alligator River across from the settlement.

The settlement was enclosed with a palisade and cannons could be seen pointing their deadly muzzles over the top of the enclosure on all sides. The Powhatans in this war party had never faced cannon in battle before and weren't aware of the carnage these weapons could inflict.

The war party stealthily moved across the river for about a half-mile up and down from the settlement. They spread out to ensure that they completely surrounded the palisade. They set up a form of communication to their chief, Ahanu, who would give orders up and down the line. The Powhatans were accomplished with giving hand signals in communicating their intentions.

Ahanu had decided to wait until night fall when the occupants within the Palisade were asleep, at their weakest and with their guards down.

Although the Tuscarora had agreed to assist the colonists in their confrontation with the Powhatans, they still hadn't left their village by the time the Powhatans had surrounded the settlement. They had agreed to put two hundred warriors in the field to support the colonists and their Croatoans friends, but were still getting prepared to march.

In the early morning hours and while it was still dark, the Powhatans attacked. They shot flaming arrows over the palisade, many of which fell into the thatched roofs of the houses and longhouses.

The men of the colony rose from their beds and went to their battle stations. They began to load the cannons and fired their harquebuses into the woods where the Powhatans were lighting their arrows. Several of the Powhatan warriors were wounded or killed on the first volley from the colonists. When one of the cannons was fired, two of the warriors were decapitated when the trunk of a tree broke off and went into a deadly spin.

The Powhatans knew that they were confronting a well-armed foe and didn't have a lot of experience fighting enemies with this kind of fire power.

Ahanu had seen enough. He signaled for the warriors to retreat. It was mid morning until they reached their canoes at the shoreline of the Pamlico Sound. They paddled back to Roanoke Island to regroup.

They had lost eleven warriors dead and five seriously wounded.

Ahanu knew that he was in way over his head.

After discussing the situation with some of the minor chiefs, it was decided to send a war party to linger in the woods around the settlement and when the colonists came out for any reason ambush them.

The other unknown that Ahanu wasn't aware of was that a Tuscarora war party of two hundred braves was moving toward the settlement to assist the colonists.

Seventy-five of the Powhatan warriors crossed back over to the mainland. After much difficulty crossing the ten miles of swampy marshland of the Croatan Peninsula, they took up positions around the settlements palisade.

A day later, they saw a flotilla of canoes coming up the Alligator River with four Tuscarora Braves in each boat. Some of the canoes stopped at the settlement, but many of the others continued up the river. The Powhatans followed by land to see where these warriors were heading. When they reached the mouth of the Alligator River and turned down the Albemarle Sound, they knew instinctively that they were heading for Roanoke Island.

The Powhatan had left about fifteen warriors on the island, most of which were wounded, and they were going to be overrun. If the Powhatans were lucky, the Tuscarora wouldn't discover the canoes that they hid after they crossed over to the mainland. They knew that if they sent a messenger to Roanoke, he would not reach the island before the Tuscarora.

Ahanu called a council of senior warriors to discuss their next move. After a lot of discussion, Ahanu made the difficult call. He decided to leave his Powhatan brothers to their fates and hold his positions around the settlement.

Ahanu also knew that they could only hold these positions for a week at the most. Furthermore, he knew that the most they could accomplish was to kill a few Croatoans and colonists.

On the third day, the gates of the palisade opened and two colonists and three Croatoans came out with fishing nets and waded into the water. As they began to net fish, the Powhatans opened up with their bows and arrows. All of the fishing party was struck by arrows, but none were fatally shot. They managed to retreat back into the palisade and secure the gates.

Now the positions of the Powhatans hiding in the woods were exposed. The colonists on the walls of the palisade opened fire into the direction where they believed the Powhatan to be hiding.

Ahanu had no choice other than to order his warriors to charge the palisade and attempt to force open its gates. It was a futile move. The cannons were primed and as soon as the Powhatan appeared from the edge of the woods the cannons opened up on them. The colonists had loaded the cannons with every kind of shrapnel that was available.

There was complete carnage among the Powhatan charging the palisades. Nearly every one of them was either killed or had a serious wound of some kind. The ones that could walk dragged their wounded and dead back into the woods.

Ahanu had a nail pierce his shoulder. It was evident to all of the Powhatans that they were defeated.

A mile into the woods they hurriedly buried their dead and continued toward the shoreline of the Pamlico Sound. The Tuscarora hadn't discovered their hidden canoes. They headed directly for the stretch of land that separated the Pamlico Sound and the Atlantic Ocean. The Powhatans were sure that the Tuscarora were waiting to ambush them at Roanoke Island.

The mouth of the Chesapeake Bay and the village of Chesepian was ninety miles away. To make matters worse, they didn't have any food or water. Ahanu instinctively knew that under these conditions many of the wounded would not make the trip to the Chesapeake alive.

The Tuscarora saw the crippled Powhatans dragging their canoes across the strip of land that separated the sound from the Ocean. They decided to leave them to escape. It was important for them to go back to the Powhatan village of Werewocomoco and inform their chief, Wahunsunacock, about the defeat that had befallen them. Maybe he'd think twice before invading the land of Croatan and the Tuscarora in the future.

When Ahanu finally made his way up the York River and into the major Powhatan town of Werewocomoco, he reported directly to the chief, Wahunsunacock, to explain the failure of the war party.

Ahanu told Wahunsunacock that he had never seen such destructive weapons that the English used against them in his life. He explained how the harquebus with one discharge can kill or wound three warriors with one shot. Ahanu further told Wahunsunacock, that the noise from the cannon was enough to have the warriors run for their lives.

"When they fired upon us with one of those weapons the earth trembled. When the smoke would clear, there were dead warriors everywhere," he said with animated gestures.

Ahanu removed his shirt and showed the nail that was still lodged in his shoulder.

"Great chief," Ahanu said. "The English cannot be defeated. To send another war party against them would be sending those warriors to their deaths. I would recommend, Great One, to let the Tuscarora deal with them. No matter which side wins, we would be the overall winner."

Wahunsunacock took the advice of Ahanu and the Powhatan

didn't have contact with the English again until they sailed up the James River in 1607.

In the fall of 1591, Ananias Dare and the small group of colonists that had joined him and Manteo on Salmon Creek were having a successful harvest. It was going to be a good year thanks to their neighbors and benefactors. The Weapemeoc Confederation had some of their warriors' assist the men hunting and the women of the tribe gave the colonist women tips on planting and caring for the budding crops.

Late one evening, Wanchese came into the colonists little village and told Ananias, as he was preparing Virginia for bed, that the chief of the Weapemeoc wanted to see all the colonist men. "The Croatoan men and Manteo are not included. The chief has something of great importance to discuss with the English," Wanchese said.

Elinor had brought Virginia home from the fields a short time before and requested that Ananias get her ready for bed while she returned to the fields. Ananias, taking Virginia with him, went from house to house around their little village collecting the seven colonist men.

When Ananias and the other colonist men entered the Weapemeoc village, they sensed something was not quite right. There were a dozen or more braves standing around the entrance of the longhouse. Ananias, Virginia, and the seven colonist men followed Wanchese to the longhouse in the middle of the village.

Wanchese stood back and held the animal skin back to allow Ananias and Virginia to be the first to walk through the door of the longhouse. As soon as they crossed the threshold, Ananias and Virginia were immediately struck sharply in the head and dragged aside. As soon as the animal skin dropped the other colonist men were immediately set upon and attacked by the braves. The seven colonists were brained by the warriors with stone clubs.

After the last colonist was murdered, Wanchese went to search for Manteo and inform him that the Weapemeoc chief had ordered the death of all the English men.

"It was unfortunate that the child, Virginia, was killed. That was an inadvertent accident," he told Manteo.

"The reasons for the killings," he continued, "were that the chief feared that the Powhatans would declare war on his confederacy for harboring the English. The chief has no desire to go to war with Powhatans."

The chief had decided to allow the women to live as long as they would take a warrior from the Weapemeoc Confederation for a husband. "You are to make the women understand why they were spared and the conditions for their not being killed," he told Manteo.

Manteo met the seven English women and Elinor coming out of the fields and he told them something terrible has happened that affected all of them.

Manteo announced the death of the English men. He explained why the chief of the Weapemeoc did what he did. He said the chief of the Weapemeoc believed that eliminating the English men was in the best interest of the confederacy and diverted an invasion by the Powhatan's.

Elinor ran to her house looking for Virginia. She instinctively knew that Ananias would not have left the child alone in the house. When she found the house empty, she knew that he must have taken her with him. She ran to the Weapemeoc Village. As she approached the longhouse where the men and Virginia had been killed, there were Indian women and warriors standing around its entrance. Seven of the men from the colony were in front of the longhouse dead on the ground.

A brave came out of the longhouse with Virginia in his arms. Blood was running from a wound to her head. She was not breathing. The brave handed the dead child to Elinor. The Indian women standing closest to Elinor supported her from collapsing.

Manteo arrived and took Virginia from Elinor. Many of the English women arrived about that same time and began to take possession of their husbands' bodies.

Many of the braves in the village assisted the English women with carrying the men's bodies back to the small colony on the Salmon River.

Ananias and Virginia's bodies were brought to the Dare's house. The English women and Elinor took turns dressing the bodies for a viewing and funeral. All the women lost their husbands, but Elinor was the only one among them who had lost a child. She was beside herself with grief.

Many of the Weapemeoc tribe came to pay their respects. Although these English colonists didn't live among them, they lived alongside their village and in many cases friendships had been established.

When Wanchese came to the Dare house, he told Elinor that the chief of the tribe was very distressed that her child, Virginia, was killed. He had ordered the braves standing just inside the door of the longhouse to brain anyone who walked through the door.

"The chief had summoned the men and not the children. In his tribe the children are always with the women. A brave would never take a child to a conference," Wanchese told Elinor.

Elinor asked Manteo and Wanchese if they would prepare graves for Ananias and Virginia far from the colony. She didn't want to see their graves every day and be reminded of that horrible situation every day.

Elinor put her skill of chiseling stone to work. She wanted to mark the graves of her husband and child.

After three days of viewing the bodies, Manteo and Wanchese moved the bodies into canoes. Wanchese rowed the body of Ananias in another canoe; Manteo rowed Elinor and the body of Virginia.

It took an hour and a half for the funeral procession to paddle the four miles to the site where Manteo and Wanchese had dug the graves the day before. The grave site was located on a little hill east of the Salmon River overlooking the Chowan River.

When they arrived at the grave site, the bodies were placed in two dugout canoes, covered with wooden lids and lowered into the pre-dug graves. Manteo and Wanchese filled in the graves and Elinor placed the stone markers at the head of each one. And then Elinor knelt down and silently said a prayer.

After a half hour at the grave sites, Elinor was led back by these two Native Americans to the canoe and then rowed back to the little settlement on the Salmon River.

The voyage of Samuel Mace was the last of Raleigh's voyages, but British merchants soon sent ships to find sassafras. The merchants sent Martin Pring to Cape Cod where Gosnold had discovered sassafras, after securing Sir Walter Raleigh's permission. Pring's objective was to gather sassafras, but was unsuccessful in locating the trees.

Queen Elizabeth's death ended recognition of Sir Walter Raleigh's charter to Virginia and his sassafras monopoly. Soon after Elizabeth's death, Raleigh was again made a prisoner in the Tower of London. After a long stay in prison, Raleigh was tried, convicted of treason, and executed.

Raleigh had discontinued sending more ships to the Alligator River with supplies years before, and the captains and crews that did go there in the beginning took a solemn oath never to reveal the location of the colonists. After a period of time and the ships stopped coming from England, the colonists spent less time collecting sassafras and more time growing crops and hunting.

As the years passed, the English colonists that lived along the Alligator River were eventually merged through marriage into the Tuscarora and Croatan cultures and spread throughout the Croatan Peninsula.

On the Chowan River in 1591 and 1592, the winter was cold, dark and depressing for Elinor. She refused to take a Native American husband as the chief of the Weapemeoc had ordered. She thought that if the chief wanted to punish her for not following his edict, it might be for the best.

In the spring of 1592, Elinor decided to write a letter to her father in the hope that he would receive it and rescue her from this nightmare by taking her back to England.

When the weather got warm that spring, she enlisted the help of Towaye to locate a stone that would be large enough to chisel a letter to her father.

They spent two days walking the shores of the Salmon River looking for just the right size stone. Towaye spotted one just off the shoreline in the water. She called out to Elinor and they waded into the water and retrieved the twenty-pound stone.

It was exactly what Elinor had been hoping to find. With some difficulty, they carried it back to Elinor's house where it was placed on the crudely built table that Ananias had constructed when they first moved from the Alligator River settlement to the Salmon River.

She spent the next several days chiseling a letter to her father, informing him of the tragedy that had befallen her and her little family. She still held out hope, however, that her father would come back to America and rescue her.

Using her skill with writing on stone she wrote:

Ananias Dare & Virginia Went Hence Unto Heaven 1591
Anye Englishman Shew John White Govr Via

Soon after you go for England, we came here. We have had only misery and war two years. About half dead before two years more from sickness, being four and twenty. Savages arrive with a message for us from a ship. A short time later they were afraid of revenge and all ran away. We believe it was not your ship. Soon afterwards the savages claim that the spirits were angry. Suddenly, they murdered all by seven. My child, Virginia, and Ananias were slain with much misery. We buried all near four miles east of this River Chowan upon a small hill. All their names are written on a rock. Put this there also. If the savages show this unto you and lead you to us, I have promised them that you will give them many presents.

EWD

Elinor spent the next year attempting to bribe the Croatoans and Weapemeoc warriors to take the stone to Roanoke Island in the hope that her father would find it. She had no way of knowing that her father, John White, passed away the year before and Raleigh had no intention of sending a rescue party to America to retrieve the colonists.

In the fall of 1592, the Weapemeoc Confederation suffered from paranoia and convinced themselves that the Powhatan's were going to launch another war party in search of the English. Since the tribe absorbed the seven English women through marriage into the tribe, excluding Elinor, the chief felt an obligation to protect them.

The elders of the tribe made a decision to move and relocate the village west toward the mountains.

Manteo came to Elinor and told her that he would take care of her. He didn't expect her to marry him, but he would protect her as if she was bonded to him. Elinor was alone and didn't have any other alternative but to accept Manteo's offer and follow along with the Weapemeoc. There is no record as to what finally became of her once the Weapemeoc left the Crowan River.

Elinor Dare has been lost to history.

It is just a matter of time, however, before the graves of Ananias and Virginia Dare are eventually found. That discovery will finally put to bed the mystery of the "Lost Colony."

EPILOGUE

The stone was found in the summer of 1937 by Louis Hammond near Edenton, NC, and it appears to hold a message from Elinor Dare to her father John White. If the stone is authentic, this stone throws a light on the fate of some of Sir Walter Raleigh's 1587 colony, popularly known as the "Lost Colony."

Hammond wrote that he found the stone, while searching for hickory nuts, three or four miles north of Edenton, about a half mile from the road, by a small bridge over water. He said he picked up the stone and carried it a short distance to the Chowan River to wash it.

He described the place as marshy with a small island, and he could see a sunken barge nearby in the river.

Although this location has previously been identified as an Indian site, which further supports this contention, this site has never previously been registered as a principle Contact-Period Indian village.

Louis Hammond took the stone to Emory University, where scientists and historians at Emory examined the stone thoroughly and could not disprove its authenticity. Despite this, they were disappointed when they went back to North Carolina with Hammond, who could not determine exactly where he had found the stone.

"He said it was about a quarter of a mile away. But after wandering a mile and a half in the swamp the professors lost patience. Finally, Hammond saw a barge grounded on the bank of the Chowan and a sand shoal nearby, he said, was where he had washed the rock. Thereafter he cleaned it with a steel brush, used an indelible lead pencil to intensify the lettering."

When Emory scientists would not participate in the purchase of the stone, History Professor Dr. Haywood Jefferson Pearce, Jr. and his father, who was President of Brenau College, purchased the stone and moved it to Brenau in Gainesville, GA.

A few years ago, a collaboration between Thomas Parramore, a North Carolina history professor at Meredith College, and the Lost Colony Center for Science and Research, Inc. resurrected an interest in the stone and brought it to NC for the first time since its discovery (unfortunately, Dr. Parramore died before this took place.)

The stone was put on tour at Roanoke Island and Edenton, NC, where it was first found. This caused a great deal of excitement, and a rebirth in interest of the 1937 discovery.

Several documentaries since that time have been attempted.

History Channel interest caused Fred Willard to take an increased interest in locating the original resting place of the stone. He enlisted the aid of Phil McMullan, a native of the area, and began to search for the place where the stone had been found. After reading all the available literature, he determined that the most important published clues to the location of the stone are:

1. The stone was found approximately four miles north of Edenton, NC
2. Hammond had just crossed a small bridge over a creek when he pulled over to gather hickory nuts and stretch his legs.

3. The stone location was a swampy place.
4. Hammond walked a short distance to the river to wash the stone.
5. When brought back to the original location with several university professors, Hammond had a hard time finding the exact location. However, he said he recognized: A small sand spit where he washed the stone, and was able to conclusively identify it because of a sunken barge on the creek.
6. Photographs of the location were taken, and soil boring samples were obtained.
7. Hammond was traveling on Rt. 17 when the discovery was made.

The location that best meets this evidence is the Cowpen Neck Road Bridge over Rocky Hock Creek. This location is approximately four miles north of Edenton and is close to the Chowan River. No other Chowan County Creek meets this description. Willard and McMullan visited the location and found the sunken barge at the mouth of the creek, near where they assumed Hammond washed the stone.

The barge Hammond referred to is today sunken just south of the mouth of Rocky Hock Creek, not in its 1937 location. Hurricanes over the past years have moved it. Conversations with local residents placed the earlier site on the Chowan River north of the creek. The area has seen extensive dredge and fill activity to accommodate a marina located on the creek. That land was swampy area in 1937, according to local residents, and much of the surrounding land is swampy now. Hickory nut shells were found in the water by the small sand spit.

Of the facts accumulated above, five have been confirmed, and only the soil boring needs to be compared and completed.

One of Hammond statements, however, cannot be as easily explained: that he was traveling on Highway 17 when the discovery was made. There is a Pembroke Creek crossing Highway 17 about two miles out of Edenton, and there was a small bridge there in 1937. However, that creek is about two miles from the Chowan River, much too long a walk while carrying a twenty-pound stone to the river to be washed.

That he was on Highway 17 when he found the stone cannot be reconciled with the other reported evidence, unless there was a desire to keep the exact location a secret. It is possible that he gave the name of the closest highway, rather than identifying an unmarked dirt road crossing Rocky Hock Creek.

It is well documented that splinter groups of the 1585 and 1587 colonies were likely living in Indian villages in the Chowan area. If the stone is authentic, one might expect it to have been found in a major Indian site—the message asks that an Indian show it to John White, whose return was expected.

Artifacts were found on the sand spit where Hammond is believed to have washed the stone, and near where the barge was located. An evaluation of the artifacts suggests that this site is Waratan, the capital village of the Weapemeoc Confederation, shown on John White's 1585 map of Virginia.

The information presented above is far from conclusive, but the research is in the early stages. A major problem with this new research is that it cannot be ascertained whether the stone was moved from another location. Because the site was the most reasonable fit to the available evidence from Hammond, it deserved further examination.

Attempts to identify 16th century artifacts at the test site have thus far been unsuccessful. Many English artifacts have been found, but they are from a later date. More excavations into deeper strata may produce such artifacts.

If authentic, the stone provides specific direction and distance to the most important gravesite yet to be found in North America: Virginia Dare and her father, Ananias Dare. The stone purported that they are buried four miles east of the location of Hammond's discovery, on a small hill. The desirable next step would be in depth archaeological studies at the site and a search for the Dare gravesites. This research will be expensive and local support will be important.

The findings to date do not yet support the authenticity of the Dare Stone. However, a prominent Golden Age Elizabethan scholar found indications in the syntax that were only used in the 16th Century.

If the stone could be authenticated, it would be the only artifact ever found related directly to the "Lost Colony." Heretofore, the single most important discovery was the Croatan site in Buxton, NC.

The Elinor Dare Stone is the first artifact discovered that directly connects to the vanished 1587 colony.

I have been given permission to see the Elinor Dare stone in September 2016 at Brenau University, Gainesville, GA. The stone is normally kept in the office of the University President. When I arrive at the University, I've been told they will take the stone out of the President's office and allow me some time to examine it. I am truly grateful to the staff of the University for this honor.

Lee Dorsey, Author

About the Author

Lee began his professional career as an actor. In his late teens, he auditioned and was cast in a Summer Repertory Company in West Virginia, the "Hilltop Players." After a summer of performing in seven plays, Lee entered college.

After attending Baltimore Junior College for two years where he received an Associate's Degree, Lee entered the American University, in Washington, D.C. to obtain a degree in Communications. While attending college, he worked part-time at WFBR Radio, writing news on the weekends. Eventually, Lee auditioned and landed an on-the-air position with Radio WANN. After college, he went to work for Radio Station WAQE, in Towson, Maryland.

Lee went to work for the United States Naval Academy in 1974 to manage their Student Union facilities. After twenty-three years, he was promoted to Director of Human Resources for the Brigade Services Division. During his tenure at the USNA, he earned two more degrees: a BS in Leadership and Management and an MS in Human Resources Management. He retired in 2008.

Lee has written several plays over the years. Most have been produced locally and professionally in Baltimore, Annapolis, and Miami. Lee has just completed a historical, two act play, titled *The Nine Day Queen*. It chronicles the story of Lady Jane Grey who was sentenced to death at the age of 17 by Queen Mary I of England. He presently is reworking the play before sending it to his publisher with offices in South Africa and London.

At this time, Lee has completed several novels. More recently, *A Forbidden Love,* published by Pink Flamingo Publications, received the National Leather Association International 2012 Writing Award Finalist–Pauline Range Award. He has written two other erotic novels. *Indiscretions* was released in November 2014, and *The Artist* was published by Pink Flamingo Publications in April 2015. Early in 2016, the novel was nominated for the Pauline Range Award. This is the second time one of his novels was honoured with this nomination.

Androgyny an Erotic Memoir was released by Torrid Books in December 2014. *A Search for Love* was released by Torrid Books on April 28, 2015. The first novel in the *Mercenaries of Panama* series (*Frank the Survivor*) was released by Christopher Matthews Publishing in 2013. The second novel in the *Mercenaries of Panama* series (*Shada*) was release by Solstice Publishing on January 20, 2015.

Lee has just finished writing a science fiction novel titled *The Triangulum Galaxy*. A contract to publish this work with Christopher Matthews Publishing was recently signed. A publication date has not been set as of this writing.

Lee now writes full time.